Book Five in the Nestled Hollow Romance series

Cover Illustration by Covers and Cupcakes

Interior Design by Mountain Heights Publishing

Author website: www.megeaston.com

"Sweet romance at its best!
I want to visit Nestled Hollow over and over again!"

-Elana Johnson
USA Today bestselling author of the *Hawthorn Harbor*
series and the *Getaway Bay* series

"Romance done right! Already looking forward to the next
Nestled Hollow love story. This series is going to be a
keeper!"

-Kimberly Krey
Best-selling author of the *Sweet Montana Brides* series

love again at the heart of
main street

love again at the heart of main street

A NESTLED HOLLOW ROMANCE

MEG EASTON

contents

Amid the din of the rainstorm beating against the roof and windows of Love a Latte, the crowd of people waiting out the storm inside the shop had to raise their voices to be heard over the storm. Since her hands were full of more drink cups and lids, Tory lifted the gate leading behind the counter with her foot so it would rise above the place that made it catch and then used her hip to swing it open.

"You know, it wouldn't take much to fix that," one of her customers, Nate Elsmore, said as he stepped up to the counter to order.

The broken gate had been bugging Tory for the past year, but not enough for it to ever get to the top of her always impressively long to-do list. She laid sleeves of cups and lids on the back counter. "And have it open without a challenge? Where's the fun in that?"

The man chuckled, and Ruth, one of her high school employees at the counter, asked him what he'd like to order. "Or would you like Tory to choose for you?"

This customer had never had Tory choose for him, so she was surprised when he requested to have Tory pick. She walked over to where he stood at the counter and studied him, a finger tapping her lips. "You are normally a one cream one sugar guy, but not this time." She squinted as she tried to see further to guess what he most needed. "Today it's a caramel macchiato."

He let out a breath of a chuckle and then turned to Ruth. "Caramel macchiato it is."

As Ruth prepared his drink, Tory grabbed the coffee pot and headed out to refresh any cups that needed it. She knew she wasn't the only one who had planned to leave before now, and knew they all might be there a while before the rain died down enough for them to leave the shop and make a run for their cars.

A good number of the tables were filled with her fellow Main Street Business Alliance members who, like her, headed over to Love a Latte after their Thursday meeting. Sadly, though, she didn't usually stay and chat like she wished she could. Her kids always spent the meeting in the back room of Love a Latte where the older two watched the younger two while one of her employees checked in on them every few minutes. By the time the meeting was over, they were more than ready to go home.

Tory refreshed the coffee for both of Nate's foremen, the mayor and Officer Banks, a couple of tables of tourists, a few high school teachers, and a few women from the Business Alliance who had pushed two tables together.

"How is everyone today?" Tory asked the table of women as she refilled the couple of cups that held regular coffee.

"We are good," Macie, the blonde-haired owner of Paws and Relax, said over the sound of pelting rain. "We were just talking shop."

Alete, one of her fellow business owners, shook her head. "We *were* talking shop until these two commandeered the conversation and got us all talking about wedding plans. Sit. We need the not-currently-engaged-to-be-married percentage to sway more in our favor."

Tory chuckled and glanced over to see that her employees had everything taken care of. She shouldn't feel guilty about sitting down for a moment—if the storm wasn't raging outside, she'd have left by now anyway. She sat down in the one empty seat and set the coffee pot on the table.

"Alete just isn't liking all the wedding talk," Whitney,

the owner of Nestled Hollow Gazette, said, "because the guy she's dating isn't challenging."

Alete raised a finger. "Correction: he doesn't challenge *me*. He's plenty challenging."

"Well, I think all the wedding mania is cute," Shelly said.

"As long as you don't do it like Joselyn did." Macie raised an eyebrow in Joselyn's direction.

"You should've seen my wedding spreadsheet," Joselyn said. "I spent so many hours poring over that."

"You had a wedding *spreadsheet*?" Tory asked, and then turned to Joselyn's sister Macie. "For real?"

Macie set her mug down, grinning. "It was color-coded and had about fifty tabs that were arranged alphabetically. There was even cross-referencing."

"And if I ever tell her that she's worrying about something too much," Joselyn said, "you better believe she doesn't let me forget it."

"What about you, Tory?" Shelly asked. "Were you a bridezilla?"

"Nope. I was barely twenty when we got engaged and still twenty when we got married. All I wanted to do was spend time with him and all he wanted to do was play, so we spent our engagement having fun. I practically let my mom plan the whole wedding. As long as I got to be married to my fiancé in the end, I didn't care."

Tory paused a moment, thinking, and then added,

"Although looking back, there were probably more than a few red flags there that I should've noticed."

"But look at how much older and wiser you are now," Alete said.

Tory snorted a laugh. "Definitely older. I don't know about wiser. I think I'm losing a few brain cells to my kids' antics daily."

"How long has it been since your divorce?" Macie asked. "Are you ready to date again?"

Tory shook her head. "A year and a half, and not even close."

Alete leaned in close, lowering her voice. "But if you were, who would you date?"

Her life was too full of running a business and being a single mom to four to have any room to daydream. Yet without having dedicated any time to thinking about it, the answer came to her mind immediately. "I would tell you, but then you'd all turn to look and that would make it awkward for everyone."

Which, of course, made everyone turn in their chairs to look anyway. There were five men around the two tables that everyone had instinctively turned to, and all five looked over when they saw the group movement. "Subtle," she said, laughing. "I'm sure that didn't make anyone uncomfortable."

"Oh, wow," Whitney said. "You're crushing on Nate?"

"Not *crushing*—I'm not fourteen. I'm not even

imagining dating him. I'm just saying he's..." Tory paused for a moment, trying to decide how to finish the sentence.

"Sweet?" Whitney suggested.

"Thoughtful?" Macie said.

"Charismatic?" Joselyn asked.

"Skilled?" Shelly added.

"Hotter than a tin can on the devil's sidewalk?" Alete said, still eyeing Nate.

"Why don't you ask him out?" Macie asked. "He's single."

There were a million reasons why she wouldn't ask anyone out. A million ways in which her divorce from Trace had left her broken and fairly certain she could never be a good wife. She rarely got a chance to just sit down and chat with other women like this, and she was enjoying herself. Still, though, not a single one of those reasons was one was she willing to share.

"Moooooom," Tory's six-year-old daughter Elodie yelled over the sound of the rain as she ran into the lobby of Love a Latte, her ten-year-old brother, Covey, right on her heels.

"Covey's being so mean!" Elodie huffed, her hands on her hips.

"She's the one being mean," Covey said, trying to keep his voice low, even though the two of them had already gotten everyone's attention. He held out his arm. "Look! She got mad and scratched me!"

"You two know not to come out here fighting. Head back into the play room and I'll be right there."

As soon as Covey and Elodie were out of earshot, Tory turned back to the women at the table. "And *that*, ladies, is exactly why nothing is going to happen in my love life." It was only a fraction of the truth, but it was enough. "Now if you'll excuse me, I need to get some very tired, very hungry kids home."

As she walked through the Employees Only door into the back rooms, she could hear arguing still coming from the play room. They'd all had a long day that had the kids, as usual, starting at Love a Latte before school, then coming straight from school to the shop, hanging out in the play room for thirty minutes, then hanging out for another hour while she was at the Main Street Business Alliance meeting, then another thirty minutes while the storm raged on. It was no wonder that they were cranky.

She shouldn't have been out in the lobby, hanging out with her fellow businesswomen while they were in the back, being checked on every few minutes but mainly being supervised by themselves. She wasn't some teenage girl, hanging out with her BFFs during the summer with no responsibilities. There were too many things she needed to be better at as a mom and as a business owner to be slacking like that.

When she opened the door to the play room, toys and

kids were strewn everywhere, and all four kids were talking, making random sounds, or banging on something.

"Mommy!" five-year-old Jackson called out as he ran to her and wrapped his arms around her legs.

"Hi, Sweetie," she said as she returned the hug. "I'm sorry I've been gone so long today. Now Covey and Elodie, tell me why you two are fighting."

They both started talking at the same time, each angry voice trying to be louder than the other. If she didn't get this solved soon, they were going to attack each other before she knew it.

"Covey, you sit over there. Elodie, you over here. Both of you, zip your lips. Aspen," she turned to her nine-year-old daughter, "do you know why they were fighting?"

"I'll tell you, Mama," Jackson said. "Since you were busy, we were playing *Tell Me About Your Day Ball* without you, and when Elodie got the ball, she said that her class did a paper where they drew what their wish is, and she drew a new dad. Because she's wishing suuuuper hard that we get a new dad. But then Covey got all mad like this," Jackson said, crossing his arms and making an angry face. "And he said that we didn't need a new dad because we already have a dad. We just need him to come back and live with us again."

Aspen rolled her eyes. "Yeah, like that's going to happen."

"So Elodie said that Dad is our dad for when we're at

his house," Jackson said, "and we need a dad for when we're home. And if he doesn't like it, then that's too bad, because she already used her wish on it."

When Jackson took a breath, Aspen took over telling the story. "And then Covey said that it didn't matter, because he used his wish on you and Dad getting back together, and since he's ten, he gets ten times the wishes—"

"—and he said because he's ten times smarter!" Elodie said in a rush before she could be reminded that she wasn't supposed to be talking.

"—and he said he's ten times smarter," Aspen confirmed, "so it'd actually be one hundred times the wishes, so his wish was going to crush her wish into oblivion."

Jackson made clawing motions with his hands. "And then Elodie jumped on Covey like she was an angry cat and scratched his arm."

Tory rubbed her forehead. She would need to talk to both Covey and Elodie about their wishes, once she had a bit more time to figure out exactly how to deal with it. And she needed to address the way they were treating each other during a disagreement. She knew that any apology they gave each other while being hungry and tired wasn't going to be genuine, so that would have to be dealt with at home, too.

She cocked her head to the side, listening. The

pounding of the rain on the building had quieted significantly. "Do you hear that? It looks like we'll be able to leave soon. Quickly, everyone, let's get these toys cleaned up so we can get out of here before the rain gets bad again."

As the five of them rushed to get the room back in order, she thought about how she could get Covey and Elodie to respect each other's different opinions, and how she could get them to show some remorse for hurting each other's feelings. Maybe if they did service for each other?

She let her employees know that she was leaving, then she and her four kids raced out the back door, jackets pulled up over their heads to keep the rain off, and hurried into their minivan.

It was times like these when she wished she had some parenting help to figure out how to best deal with issues like this. When she and Trace had gotten divorced, she'd lost both a business partner and a parenting partner. In truth, she'd been losing both for a while before that, so she was no stranger to doing things on her own.

But still, she wished she had someone to tell her how she was supposed to let Covey and Elodie know that neither of them was going to be getting their wishes.

"Did you get hold of Southwark Construction?" Nate asked Donna during his weekly post-Business Alliance meeting with his two foremen. "When can we get their guys over here?"

He took a sip of his drink as the rain pounded down outside the window they sat next to. He'd only tried a caramel macchiato once before and had hated it, but today it hit the spot. Maybe he should have the coffee shop owner choose for him more often.

Donna shifted in her seat. "You're not going to like this. DeKirk Construction saw how desperate people are for construction companies statewide right now, so they opted for the bigger paycheck and headed to Colorado Springs. Southwark is scrambling to pick up all the contracts DeKirk defaulted on, so they don't have enough guys as it is. They no longer have any to lend us."

Nate shook his head. Companies like DeKirk that showed no integrity drove him nuts. Nate's name was the one on their trucks. That meant something to him. It meant he did anything he needed to in order to finish jobs on time and to do a job that he was proud of. Leaving all those people with partially finished houses was just about as unethical as it got.

He pulled out their most updated list of construction projects—where each one was currently at, what sub-contractors were lined up, and what needed to be done still—and ran a hand through his hair. "Okay, so here's where we're at. If we can't get help from Southwark, where does that leave us?"

"I've searched high and low for more people," Donna said. "There just aren't any. Construction is booming through the whole state right now, and everyone's taken."

His brother, Beckett, shook his head. "To meet our deadlines, we're going to have to open our guys to unlimited overtime, and probably even offer bonuses for completion or for working a certain amount of overtime."

Construction was booming, yet Elsmore Construction wasn't likely to even turn a profit if they had to spend so much on man hours. But meeting deadlines was more important than profits. And at least the extra pay would make his guys happy. He took a deep breath and gave a curt nod. "Let's do it then."

The rain picked up even more, making the sound in the overly-crowded shop even louder. He had a home ready for footings and one ready for framing. This rain was going to slow both projects. But, he reminded himself, he had a good crew. They were dependable, skilled, and hard-working. They could pull this off.

"It looks like Casey's soccer game isn't going to happen today," Beckett said, looking out the window at the downpour. "The kid's going to be crushed."

Nate loved watching his little four-year-old nephew play. Their field was teeny and some of the kids were just as content to chase butterflies as they were to chase the ball, which made it even more fun to watch.

He wished he had a little soccer player of his own. But even though he'd tried to convince his ex-wife during the entire five years they'd been married that they should have kids, he'd never managed to get her to agree. "Maybe he'll need his favorite uncle to bring over ice cream tonight to console him."

"*If* we can ever get out of here," Donna said, frowning at the storm.

Rain was running down the road in a river that stretched from the sidewalk to the creek that ran down the middle of Main Street, splitting the road in two. It had probably been a dozen years since he'd last seen a rainstorm this bad.

"I say we just make a run for it," Nate said. "My pack's waterproof, and I've got to get to my computer to rework the schedules to include overtime, and you both need to get home to your families. We have a busy construction season ahead of us—you better grab the time with them while you can." He picked up his bag and started putting his papers in it. "I'm not afraid of getting a little wet."

"Me, neither," Beckett said, putting his papers in his pack.

"You're both crazy," Donna said, but she was packing up her things as well.

Once Nate got all of his schedules and plans back into his pack, he put on his jacket, grabbed a lid for his cup, and then headed toward the door. As if the weather was looking out for him, the rain lessened considerably, the cacophony quieting in the shop.

Everyone else in the shop must have decided this might be their best chance at leaving anytime soon, too, so they all crowded around the doors with him. He grinned at Donna and Beckett, said goodbye, and then they, along with everyone else in Love a Latte, raced to their vehicles. Even though the rain had slowed, it was still coming down enough that he got soaked in the five or six seconds it took him to make it from the door of the coffee shop to his truck.

Once he got inside the cab, he brushed the rain off his hair and suppressed a full-body shiver as he started his truck and turned the heat on full blast. Then he pulled out of his parking spot and headed down Main Street.

He did a U-turn on the bridge over Snowdrift Springs at Center Street and had just turned onto the other side of Main Street and the direction of his office when his hair stood on end. A microsecond later, he slammed on his brakes as a blindingly bright flash lit up the sky, street, and buildings, and a crack split the air so loudly he felt it reverberate in his chest.

The flash was gone as quickly as it had come, but the image had been burned into his retinas. It didn't take long for his eyes to adjust before he saw what the lightning had struck—the towering tree in the small outdoor play area between Love a Latte and City Hall, and he froze. The lightning split the tree right down the middle, and one of the halves was slowly tipping toward Love a Latte.

Nate stepped on the gas, like getting back there faster would make a difference, racing toward the coffee shop as the massive section of tree reached an angle where gravity pulled it down faster and faster. He screeched to a stop across Snowdrift Springs from the coffee shop right as the tree crashed down onto the building.

The sound was deafening as it crashed through the wood, brick, glass, and front doors, toppling the pillars at the sides holding up the roof overhang, and eventually landing on the cement sidewalk in a reverberating *thud*, a mess of branches and broken building in a chaotic heap. Nate pulled out his phone and called Beckett as he raced over the pedestrian bridge and to the building.

Beckett answered on the first ring. "What was that noise?"

"Lightning struck the tree by Love a Latte, and it fell on the building. You've got the tarps in your truck, right? Bring them. Call Donna and have her round up a dozen sheets of plywood and get them here as quickly as she can." Nate hung up the phone and stuck it in his pocket. No need to call 911— the police station was two buildings down and the fire station next to it, so they already knew.

He ran to where he could see through the wreckage of tree and building, holding a hand over his eyes to keep the incessant rain from impairing his vision as much and trying to find a spot where he could see inside the building. "Is everyone in there okay?"

Ruth, the girl who had served him his coffee, moved into view, clutching Katie, the other girl who had been working. "We're okay." Her voice came out shaky and terrified.

"Was anyone else inside?"

Katie shook her head. "Just us."

"Everything's okay now. All the damage is done— you're going to be okay."

They both nodded, and Nate's attention was pulled

toward a minivan racing up to him and stopping right in the middle of the street. Tory got out of the driver's seat, shock and disbelief all over her face, and put a trembling hand over her mouth. She looked so broken and vulnerable and horrified, he wanted to put his arms around her and calm all her fears. They didn't know each other well, but he knew she probably just needed someone— anyone— to reach out.

But her kids got out of the van right then and immediately surrounded her, clutching on to her for comfort and protection. Tory's posture immediately became one of commanding strength. People from the buildings all around came out in the pouring rain to see what had happened. Brooke, the woman who owned Best Dressed, came running over and Tory asked her to take her kids and get them somewhere dry. It had only taken seconds from when she'd first come to a stop to when she was by his side, trying to see inside.

"Ruth? Katie? Are you two okay?"

"We are a little freaked out," Katie said, still clutching Ruth. "But we're safe."

He could tell that Tory was a fraction of a moment away from plowing her way through the wreckage to get to the girls. "We're coming in to get you," Nate said, and he and Tory started climbing over the tree.

There were several places where they had to grab hold of each other for support as they stepped somewhere unstable or slippery from the rainstorm. And there were a few times when they had to hold sections of the wall out of the way so they could climb through, all while rain poured down from the sky, soaking them to the bone.

"Watch out for the broken glass," Tory said, nodding to the remains of the window Nate had been sitting next to less than five minutes earlier.

"Don't step there," he said as he pulled Tory toward him. He'd noticed that the section of the door that she'd just put a foot on was balancing precariously on a piece of wood that was about to break. She stepped on top of a pile of broken bricks instead. They ducked under a beam and were finally inside.

Tory immediately ran to the two girls and wrapped them in a hug, then stood back, inspecting them for harm. And then she leaned forward and hugged them again. "Ruth, you are shaking! Katie, where were you two when the tree hit?"

"She was walking over to that table to wipe it off." The girl pointed to the table that was now smashed under pieces of the building. "The ceiling nearly crashed down on top of her. I was behind the counter."

The entire front of the building was gone, lying in a heap under the massive tree. Rainwater poured onto the floor of the shop, gathering in puddles. Nate went to the biggest opening where he could see through the wreck to the people on the street and called out to them. "Is Steve or Jordan coming?"

"They're almost here," someone yelled back, and a moment later, he saw the two EMTs jog up to the open space.

"Both girls are safe," he told them, "but at least one of them may be going into shock. I'll let you in through the back door."

Nate hadn't been in the back rooms of Love a Latte, but he knew enough about building code to know it had to have a back door. He guided the three of them through the Employees Only door as Tory called Ruth's mom to have her meet them there.

When they passed a room filled with toys, Tory reached inside and grabbed a blanket from a shelf in the room, and wrapped it around the girls. Nate saw a second blanket, grabbed it, and wrapped it around Tory. She was so soaked that rain was dripping from her clothes and hair, and she had just seen the front of her building collapse. She was probably freezing and close to going into shock herself.

Once the paramedics got the girls out of the building and Nate flipped the breaker to make sure they didn't have any issues with possible exposed wires, Nate walked with Tory back to the lobby that was no longer the comforting place to hang out that it once was. They both stood side-by-side, staring at the shambles of the building and the water that was still coming in.

He heard a quick intake of breath and looked over at Tory to see that a tear was rolling down her cheek, her breath hitching. She stood unmoving. "If anyone had stayed a few minutes longer..."

This time he didn't second guess himself— he could see she needed comfort, so he wrapped an arm around her shoulders and said, "Everyone's safe. The building can be repaired and everyone's safe."

He stood next to her for several long minutes, holding tight as she looked at the front of her store that was now in ruins and cried.

three

TORY

By the time Tory got the last kid in bed and they had finally fallen asleep, she wanted to collapse. Thankfully, when her friend Brooke had taken her kids, she had noticed that they were starving and that it hadn't been helping their ability to cope with what they'd seen. So she took the kids to Back Porch Grill where Cole made them dinner.

By the time they had all gotten back home, it was well past their normal bedtimes. But even though they were exhausted, they still had the remains of the adrenaline pumping through them.

Their bedtime ritual had been hijacked by questions about the storm and the tree and the coffee shop and what was going to happen. She knew they weren't likely to be able to calm themselves enough to sleep until they got their questions answered, so she answered them all and put them to bed. And then put them to bed again. And again and again.

Elodie and Jackson were understandably terrified of the storm that was still not done dumping water on their little town and were afraid that a tree might come crashing into their house.

Aspen wanted to run through every escape scenario she could think of, in case something dangerous happened when they were at home, school, or at the coffee shop. Luckily, Tory was able to calm the nine-year-old girl down enough that they didn't have to practice drills that night in the rain. But she had stayed up the latest of all of them, using a flashlight shining on her notebook, drawing maps of each location and which ways they would run in an emergency, what they would grab, where they would meet, and setting up a buddy system to make sure everyone made it out.

And of course, Covey was worried about what they were going to do for money with Love a Latte in no shape to open anytime soon. His questions were the most difficult to answer because Tory worried about the exact same thing.

And that was why, even though it was nearing midnight and she hadn't managed to get warm again after being soaked in rain that froze her to her core, she was sitting at her kitchen table, making lists of what she needed to do tomorrow. Of all the people she needed to call, all the things she needed to check on, and all the research she needed to do.

As she thought through each thing, she found her mind wandering to that moment inside the shop once Katie and Ruth had left. Once she'd had a chance to really look at the damage done, the impact of it had truly hit her. She'd felt herself breaking at that moment, but Nate had stepped in and wrapped his arm around her, holding her together.

He didn't freak out about the damage. He didn't start saying what they needed to do next. He didn't tell her everything was going to be fine. He had just held her tight. For that one moment, she was able to feel the emotions that were crashing down upon her and didn't have to pretend to be strong for anyone. He hadn't expected anything out of her; he had just held her. It was a gift she had sorely needed.

They had only stood there together for one or two minutes before people started pouring in to help, but it had been enough that she could be strong again when she needed to be.

Nate had apparently asked his brother to bring tarps because it wasn't long before there were ladders against the broken edges of her building and men were tying them up, keeping the bulk of the water out of her building. A dozen people had come inside to help her clean up the river of rainwater so it wouldn't do any further damage.

And before they were done, another dozen or so people were nailing plywood as best as they could over the bigger openings, so at least the building would be somewhat safe from any intruders bigger than a raccoon. Of course, she had seen what kind of damage a raccoon could do. But she wasn't going to worry about that. She already had enough worries piled on her plate.

She shoved her lists aside. Her mind might not settle down anytime soon, but today had been three weeks long and her body was crashing fast. She needed to get to bed before it just decided it was going to collapse wherever she happened to be at the moment.

———

If Tory had ever wondered if she had made the right choice when she went with a local insurance company, she got her answer when they had gotten an insurance adjuster to come to the shop the very next afternoon.

"I figure you need this quickly," the balding man said, taking a seat at one of the tables that hadn't been destroyed. "I can get all my calculations finished tonight and have it into the insurance company by the time they open tomorrow."

"Thank you," Tory said, an exhale of relief coming out

with the words as she sunk into the chair across from him. She hadn't exactly had any spare money since the divorce a year and a half ago, and that had drained her savings. She was worried enough about paying the insurance deductible; she had no idea what she was going to do with the coffee shop closed, especially if it was going to be for long.

"Once they approve it, which should only take a day or two, you can start moving on things pretty quickly. If you can."

Everything had sounded good until those last three words. "What do you mean, *if I can?*"

The man shrugged. "Finding a construction company right now isn't going to be easy— there's a bit of a shortage. You might need to prepare yourself that this," he motioned at the conditions of the front of the building, "is the way things are going to be here for a while."

He left her with her copy of the paper that said he'd performed the inspection and when the report would be filed with the insurance company, along with a number to call if she didn't hear from them by the next afternoon. Tory didn't know how long she'd sat there in her damaged building, wind whistling through the gaps in the plywood, eyes unable to focus on the paper, her mind a foggy place where she couldn't seem to find a direction to start heading.

She was pulled out of her haze by a knock at the back

door. Maybe it was one of her employees, coming to get something they forgot or to get a fresh look at the damage. She stood, straightened her shirt, headed toward the back of her building, and opened the door. Nate stood there, wearing his usual construction outfit— jeans, t-shirt, work boots, and a tool belt— and looking as fine as ever. He was like the sun chasing away the clouds that had settled in this afternoon.

"Hi," she said. "Um, come on in."

It was awkward to just stand in the hall with this man who somehow seemed larger now that she'd admitted out loud that she found him date-worthy. *If* she was going to find anyone date-worthy, which she very much wasn't. Being married to Trace for ten years had been more than enough relationship for a very long time.

She didn't want to face the front of the store again yet, but the only other place to invite him would be the play room that doubled as her office, where the only place to sit other than her office chair was an exercise ball or rocking horse. Or the stock room, but that seemed a little too cozy.

So they went to the front again.

Nate looked at the damage and checked the plywood. "It looks like this is holding up pretty well. Has any more rain gotten in?"

"No. Your foremen did a great job. I should've already been by to thank you for all your help last night." She felt vulnerable saying it, but she made herself add, "And thanks for holding me when the gravity of the situation fully hit me. I couldn't have guessed how much I would need that kind of support."

Nate tensed and immediately found the missing beams at the top of the broken area super interesting.

Nice job making things awkward, Tory. She shouldn't have said anything.

He cleared his throat. "No problem. Glad I could help."

He pushed on a few areas of the plywood, probably testing how sturdy they seemed, and then he turned to her. "I just wanted to check in to see how everything was going."

"Oh, you know. For a while now I've been thinking of bringing some of the outdoors in to make the place feel fresher. I had imagined a few succulents in the windowsills, but clearly, this is the universe's way of telling me that I wasn't thinking big enough."

Nate smiled. "The fresh air is nice. It's more ventilated than any other shop on Main. I bet if you petitioned the Keetchs, they'd give you a *Most Breezy Business on Main Street* plaque with the Main Street Business Alliance logo at the top. You could hang it on the wall right there."

There was a reason why Nate's name had popped into Tory's head so quickly when Alete had asked. He just seemed to get her.

But she wasn't looking for someone to get her. She couldn't imagine herself looking to date again— ever. Everything about her was a mess. She was in no shape to be anyone's wife, girlfriend, or even their date for the evening. Maybe she should shout *that* to the universe.

She tapped a finger on her lips and nodded. "That's a great idea. I should ask— it would go well with the decor."

"Besides hanging out in here, admiring the unplanned renovation and the beauty and craftsmanship that went into these sheets of plywood, how are things? Is your insurance company cooperating?"

"Yep—they're fabulous. Ten out of ten. I highly recommend."

He nodded. "That's good. But?"

She didn't want to complain to Nate about her discouragement over her prospects of finding a contractor. He was the only contractor based in Nestled Hollow and he was too busy to take on another job for sure— everyone said that Elsmore Construction was the best in this part of the state. If she complained, it would likely just make him feel bad that he couldn't help.

"Tory?"

He was looking at her with concerned eyes like he knew there was more that she hadn't been willing to say. Curses! Why did he have to be so good-looking, charming, *and* perceptive?

But maybe he would have some insider knowledge that

would help her know where to turn. Like staring off into space when the insurance adjuster left had proven, she would probably stay pretty lost without someone giving a suggestion. "The adjuster mentioned how busy every contractor in the state was right now. I'm guessing that's true?"

Nate sighed and nodded. "We're so far over-booked this year that we'll be scrambling to make our deadlines. Everybody's in the same boat."

"There isn't some kind of global waiting list, is there?"

"No, but that's a brilliant idea that someone should make happen."

Tory wandered toward the register and the coffee machines, hands on her hips, and then turned back. "When do things normally slow down for the year?"

"Depends on the weather. Most companies book through October, so if we get behind, we can work into early November. Every once in a while the weather holds out and we work into December."

"So I would need to wait seven months from now for a possible opening?" She collapsed into the nearest chair and dropped her face into her hands. What was she going to do? She didn't get child support— Trace had left her Love a Latte in lieu of having the responsibility of holding down a job. This shop was her family's sole source of income, and she couldn't go without its income for seven months or more.

Besides, if she left everything unused and in a building open to the elements for that long, all the equipment would likely no longer be usable. All her stock would be trash. Whatever the insurance company decided to give her wouldn't be enough if she had to wait that long for repairs.

If she kept thinking along those lines, she was likely going to fall into a pit of despair, and this kind man did not need the awkwardness of watching her fall apart again. She lifted her head and could see that he was already looking at her, conflicted, wondering if maybe she was going to cry and if he should do something.

She was strong. She was fierce. Getting through her divorce and a year and a half of single parenting was worse than this. This she could handle. She sat up straight, put her shoulders back, and then stood.

"Do you know what?" she said. "This isn't unsolvable. People in this town still need their coffee. I will cut a door in that plywood, screw some hinges to it, borrow a chainsaw and cut a pathway in the tree, and clean up the broken glass and bricks. The broken building is practically a tourist attraction. I'll just take a cart through my homemade doorway and sell coffee from the street. The novelty will probably attract even more customers than normal."

Nate nodded. "That sounds like a solid plan. You could even take a couple of your tables and chairs outside and there can be an outdoor seating area on the sidewalk beneath the boughs of the fallen tree."

"And then I could ask the Keetchs if they could give me a plaque for *Best Use of Natural Surroundings*. I could hang it on the rubble outside."

"You'd have a line of customers down the street once the rest of the county heard about that award."

"Business would probably be booming so much that by the time November came around, I wouldn't want the building fixed after all."

Nate laughed. "And when that time comes, I will personally come and help you to build an igloo over your outdoor seating area."

"Deal."

Tory smiled. The light conversation was exactly what she needed to get her head on straight again, quit wallowing, and believe she could make a plan.

NATE

Nate had stopped by Love a Latte expecting two things: to find a discouraged woman despairing, and to get a better look at the damage done than what he'd gotten last night. What he hadn't expected was to see someone showing so much strength and who could still joke around. He had asked his sister Jeigh to come with him so she could console Tory while he tried to inconspicuously check things out, but she hadn't been able to get away from work. He'd almost talked himself out of going, but he was glad he hadn't.

He also knew that no matter how strong Tory seemed, or how good of an attitude she had, she still needed help. Last night, as she'd first witnessed the damage from the street and when it had all hit her a few minutes later inside, he'd seen on her face just how much losing this shop affected her and how serious it was.

And it wasn't just Nestled Hollow or western Colorado or the state of Colorado that was in a construction boom right now. It was all the surrounding states, too, so there was no chance of her getting a construction company to take her shop on anytime soon.

Nate pulled out his construction notepad. He made some sketches and notes as he sat in his truck, glancing at the outside of the building whenever he needed to verify something.

There were some very long days ahead of him with the projects that Elsmore Construction was already committed to, but he could probably help Tory after work. He'd be exhausted from putting in so many hours a day, especially since it was all such physical work, but it wouldn't be forever— at the pace he'd have to go, probably a couple of months. He could handle it for that long. She needed help, and he was the one best equipped to help.

Tapping the pen on his notepad, he looked back up at the building, then down at his notes. So much of it, especially tearing things out and re-framing the building, were things he couldn't do as just one person, though. He'd need help. He couldn't go to Beckett or Donna— he already felt terrible about how much they would have to be away from their families in the coming months. He couldn't ask them to give up the little bit of time they had with them.

He couldn't go to his crew, either. They were all in the same boat as Donna and Beckett.

But maybe he could go to the townspeople. He mostly needed willing bodies and helping hands, and he could direct them even if they had no experience. It had only been a year since he'd moved back to Nestled Hollow, and although he'd only had a few conversations with Tory, he'd seen her help out this town plenty of times. Surely they would be on board to return the favor.

He turned the key in the ignition of his truck and headed toward Elsmore's Market. He might not be the best at knowing who to ask or how to organize the asking, but his parents were. They owned the only market in town, so they knew everyone.

When Nate walked into the market, his dad was smiling and chatting with Mrs. Davenport at the register as he rang up her groceries and his mom was back in produce, whistling while she put out some avocados. He helped his dad carry Mrs. Davenport's groceries to her trunk, and then the two of them headed back into the store.

His mom gave him a hug. "Hello, Son! Strange to see you in the middle of the day. Are you here shopping?"

Nate leaned against the display of apples. "Actually, I wanted to ask for your help." He explained what Love a

Latte needed and what kind of help he was hoping to get from the town. "And, I was hoping that you two would be willing to line up the help."

"Sure thing, Son," his dad said. "I'll ask everyone who comes in and make a few calls between customers."

"And I can ask the Helping Hands group at church to pass the word on. When do you want help?"

Nate had thought about this. He desperately needed to work every Saturday during the construction season. His whole crew did. But the first step at Love a Latte—removing the tree and all the debris from the building, along with the parts of the building that were still attached but too destroyed to use—would take the largest number of people and Saturday would be the day to get the biggest crowd to help.

"How about tomorrow morning at ten?" He could just plan to be at his first site before dawn, get four hours of work in, then work with whoever his parents could line up last minute, and then work at one of his sites until it was too dark to see. "And then I could use help framing Monday evening."

His dad went up to the phone by the registers to start calling people, and his mom started placing oranges in their spot. Nate turned to her. "Will you let me know if you can get people to come? Then I'll let Tory know that we have a plan."

She tossed an orange to him and he added it to the bin. "I'm getting the sense you might like this girl."

It wasn't hard to see that she was a beautiful woman; he'd noticed that plenty of times. And when Tory had thanked him for holding her last night, there was something that passed between them— he was attracted to her and he was pretty sure she was attracted to him. But he got the vibe that she wasn't looking for a relationship. And neither was he. In different circumstances, maybe.

"She's just someone who needs help, and like you always told us, 'If you can help, you should.'"

"That's my boy," she said, patting his arm, and then pulled out her phone.

———

It wasn't even six o'clock before Nate got a call from his dad, saying that he had gotten a dozen people committed to being at Love a Latte in the morning with gloves, ready to work, and another handful were planning to meet him on Monday night. With help like that, this plan could work. His crew was doing well on the home they were working on, so he headed over to his office and typed up a proposal, then drove straight to Tory's house.

Just as he was pulling in front of her house, her kids were running out to a sedan in her driveway, waving at the man driving. Their dad, maybe? He was suddenly unsure about walking up to the door. But Tory was standing on the porch and had already seen him. When he hesitated, she waved at him to come up. He took one glance at the man, and the look the man gave back wasn't a friendly one.

Nate got out of the car and strolled up to the house as he heard car doors shutting behind him.

"Hi," he said.

"Hi. What brings you here? Oh no." Tory grabbed a stuffed giraffe off a table by the door and ran out to the car that was pulling out of the driveway. "Elodie! You forgot Pickles Shakespeare the Fifty-Tooth!"

Her daughter rolled down her window, and when Tory handed her the giraffe, the little girl hugged it to her chest.

When Tory came back to the porch, Nate said, "I'm guessing that was their dad?"

"Yeah. They sleep over at his house on Friday nights. Come in."

It must've been tough getting everything ready for the kids to leave, because Tory ran her fingers through her hair, then exhaled a deep breath as she sunk into a chair at her kitchen table and motioned for him to sit.

A cat immediately started rubbing up against his leg, and Tory looked toward the pantry. "Oh, Cleopatrick. Did Aspen forget to feed you before she left?" She got up and opened a can of cat food and put it into the cat's dish, and set it on the floor near the pantry door.

"Have you found a construction company?" He already knew the answer, but thought he should ask before offering.

She shook her head. "And I called everyone. I mean *everyone.*"

Nate nodded. "I have a proposal." He set the papers down on the table.

A dog ran into the kitchen and straight to the cat's food dish. "No, Nacho," Tory said, scooping it up and sitting back in her chair, the dog on her lap.

Tory raised a curious eyebrow and pulled the papers toward her. He watched her expression as her eyes skimmed the paper. Surprise, disbelief, confusion. Then her eyes flashed up to meet his. "I don't understand."

"You need your shop working as soon as possible."

"True."

"People need their coffee."

She nodded. "It's vital." She lifted the top paper to glance at the one below it. "But how?"

"The town is showing up at ten tomorrow morning, and we're going to clear away the debris. Monday some are going to come help frame. That will cover the bulk of the work that has to be done by more than one person."

"And the rest?"

"That will be done by me in the evenings."

She studied him for a long moment and he tried to guess what she was thinking. Then she pushed the papers back across the table. "I can't."

He pushed them back. "You can." Past experiences had made him think she'd have been thrilled. He hadn't expected a no. But from what he knew of Tory, maybe he should have guessed.

"Nate," she said and breathed out slowly. "Just because you're the only contractor in Nestled Hollow doesn't mean this is your responsibility."

"No, but it does mean that I can help. I might be the only one in the state who can take on the project. I know someone in the county office who can get your building permit rushed through so we can start repairs soon. And everyone in town seems more than willing to help as much as needed. Love a Latte is practically the beating heart of Nestled Hollow. Nobody wants to see it gone."

"Because everyone needs a beating heart."

"Exactly."

She shook her head, set the dog down on the floor, then stood and walked to her patio doors, looking out at her back yard. Her dark hair fell in waves just below her shoulders, and it shocked him to realize that he wanted to touch it. To run his fingertips across those strong shoulders that seemed to be able to hold up so much. She was wearing an unadorned navy t-shirt and faded jeans, and her silhouette against the evening sun took his breath away.

He looked down at the proposal sitting on the table so he'd stop admiring her. Was he really going to have to sell this idea? Pitch his company? Provide references? Maybe so. This was her business, after all. Her livelihood. She probably wanted to make sure things got done right, not just to call it done. Maybe she wasn't okay with a lot of the initial work being done by unskilled workers.

He could understand her hesitation. If this had been his business, he wouldn't have gone with a contractor who showed up on his doorstep saying he could take the job. He would've researched, checked out each contractor, talked to people, and found the best one. But she didn't have that luxury unless she was willing to wait at least seven months. Or, in reality, probably until next spring for many companies.

But he also knew that the company he had built from the ground up was among the very best. She wasn't going to find another who would do a better job, and she definitely wouldn't find it anytime soon.

"I pride myself on doing good work. I wouldn't be willing to take on this job if I didn't think that I could do it well. I can give you a list of all the homes and businesses I've built in the area in the past year and in Denver before that so you can research."

She turned around and looked at him, still silent. *Oh*

no. Nate could call it what he wanted, but he realized as he looked at her that it was abundantly clear that what he was experiencing wasn't just admiration— it was downright attraction. That was not good. Attraction always ended badly.

What was he thinking, trying to push this? Doing this project would turn his life upside down in every possible way. His life over the next six months was going to be overly busy as it was. He didn't need a complication like this.

He shouldn't be here. He should be doing everything he could to run far away from this project. He stood and picked up the proposal. "I know a couple of builders who do solid work and are pretty careful to make sure they don't overbook. They'd be your best shot at getting an earlier construction time. I'll send you their contact information." He turned to leave.

"Nate."

He halted and then turned back to Tory.

"I've seen the work your company does. If I had my pick of builders, I'd go with Elsmore Construction."

Her words made his chest lighten in a way he hadn't expected. "But?"

"But it would be asking so much of you that money would never be able to repay. This is going above and beyond what I could ever ask."

"You aren't asking; I'm offering. The whole town is."

What was he doing? He could've just said *I understand* and walked away.

But could he have? Could he walk away and every day see Love a Latte in ruins, desperately needing help, knowing that he could be the one to help but not doing anything? Probably not.

Emotions flashed across Tory's face, but they were so quick and she was obviously trying to hold them back, so he couldn't quite read what they were. Then she swallowed, gave a slight nod, and with her eyes fixed on his, whispered, "Thank you."

five

TORY

L ike she did every Friday night for the last several weeks after Trace picked up the kids, Tory drove to see her mom in Littleton. Since her mom's crash that left her with a boot on her foot, a sling on her arm, a couple of broken ribs, and quite a bit of bruising, she came on Friday evenings to grocery shop, help around the house, and care for her mom.

Tory unlocked the front door and walked inside. "Hi, Mom," she called out as she headed toward the kitchen. She found her sitting at the table, finishing up the grocery list. Tory leaned down and hugged her.

"I can't believe that you had a tree struck by lightning that fell and destroyed your shop!"

She sat in the chair next to her mom and nodded. "It's been kind of crazy."

"And I can't believe I had to hear it from Christene and not you."

"Christene was here? I thought she came on Tuesdays."

Her mom sighed, reached her good arm out, and placed her hand on Tory's shoulder. "She used the phone, dear. I can't believe you'd let your sister know something big like that, but you'd leave your mom in the dark."

"It happened last night, Mom, so I decided telling you in person was better than a phone call." She had told Christene the news when she had called to chat moments before the insurance adjuster had shown up to appraise the damage. Now she wished she would've thought to ask her not to tell their mom yet.

"How bad is it?"

"Pretty bad. The entire front of the store is destroyed."

"Are you going to get it fixed soon? I've heard there's a shortage of construction workers."

"Miraculously, yes."

"By someone good? I've heard there are a lot of shoddy construction companies out there. You don't want your foundation shifting and putting cracks in your walls like my friend Cynthia's daughter's did."

"They're good, Mom." She stood up and went behind her mom, rubbing next to her shoulder blades where they always seemed to ache lately.

Her mom relaxed and leaned forward on the table,

resting her head on her arms. "I swear you have magic hands, Tory." After a few moments of silence, her mom said, "Maybe you should start giving massages to the good-looking single guys who come into your shop. Once they find out how magical your touch is, I bet they'd all be interested."

Tory laughed out loud. "Mom. Oh my goodness, Mom. I can't believe you just said that."

"I just want you to be happy and in love again."

"That would be great, I'm sure. But Mom, you know I'm way too messed up for a relationship. My 'magical touch' isn't going to get a guy to overlook everything else."

Her mom sat quietly for a moment as Tory rubbed her back. Then, with her forehead still resting on her arms and her voice coming out muffled, she said, "So this construction company you miraculously found to fix the damage. Are there any cute single guys working for them?"

"I'll tell you what. If one of the people who comes to work in my shop is an attractive single guy who's looking for an obstinate, intimidating, jaded thirty-two-year-old woman *and* an insta-family, complete with a cat, a dog, a gerbil, 4 chickens, and 5 fish, I will let you know before I tell Christene."

———

Instead of keeping the kids until noon like he usually did on Saturdays, Trace texted at nine and said he had some homes to show that morning and would need to bring the kids back at ten. Which, of course, was right when people were going to be showing up at Love a Latte to help.

She sighed, knowing that any requests to bring them back a little early so she could get them ready to go help or a little later so she could get things going at the shop were going to fall on deaf ears. So she just texted back and asked him to drop them off at Love a Latte instead of home, and then she gathered up the work gloves they were going to need. Then she threw a few extra pairs of socks into the bag because it was a chilly day and they were kids and Trace was Trace.

She had called Joey's Pizzas and Subs after leaving her mom's the night before to see if he could make some giant subs to feed the people who were coming to help, and he gave her a discount that had blown her away. She got a little choked up when she stopped by to pick them up and he loaded her back seat full of so many sandwiches for how little she had paid.

After racing to the shop and taking trip after trip to haul the sandwiches and a few bags of ice from her van through the back door and to the fridges in her shop, she started making coffee and hot chocolate. She didn't know how many people were going to come and help, but they were likely going to be cold in this weather, and the least she could do was to start them off with something warm.

Once she had all the cups filled and on a rolling cart, she pushed it out the back door of the shop. She was surprised at how many cars were in the back parking lot, with more pulling in. She waved at all of them and walked alongside Don Anderson and Bo Charleston as they all made their way down the access road between Love a Latte and the hair salon.

The end of the road was blocked by the top of the tree that had fallen, so Don picked up one side of the cart and she picked up the other, and they carefully stepped over the branches and set the cart down on the front sidewalk.

People were walking toward the building from both directions of Main Street, and she was suddenly overcome by everyone's generosity. Nate and his brother Beckett had already gotten a truck and trailer maneuvered into place to haul off the debris, the trailer detached and off to the side, the truck positioned to pull the tree away from the store.

She walked over to Nate, who was pulling big thick straps out of the truck box in the back of his truck, his flexed muscles showing through his flannel shirt. She looked around the crowd of at least three dozen men, women, and teens. "You weren't kidding about people needing their coffee."

Nate laughed, and she realized how much she loved

the deep rumbling sound. "They don't call it 'survival juice' for nothing."

"Thank you for organizing all of this."

"Thank my parents next time you go to Elsmore's Market. They're the ones who got everyone here."

Tory smiled at him, knowing that there was a lot more to it than getting everyone to come. "Well, I guess it's time we get this party started." Nate's tailgate was down, so she took a big step up onto the bumper and then into the back of his truck. Nate climbed up right behind her. At that height, she could see everyone so much better, and they all quieted quickly and turned to look at her.

She looked around at all the faces. There were customers she'd helped daily. Some she only saw in the store every few weeks. People from church. People from Main Street businesses. People from her kids' school. People from throughout Nestled Hollow, and it made her voice catch in her throat.

"Thank you, everyone, for coming to help. It's a big job, and it means a lot to me that you came to help with it." She wished she had the words to fully convey the gratitude she felt in her heart for their willingness. It meant so much more than she had the words to say. But she knew they probably didn't want her to stand up there and get all emotional and sappy, either.

So she cleared her throat. "Now I know you all don't want to spend all day out here in the cold, so we better get going. Grab yourself some coffee or hot chocolate if you haven't already, then I guess we should split up into about three teams." She looked at all the damage that needed to be cleared away. "Probably one to deal with the tree, one for the big stuff, and one for the smaller."

From the corner of her eye, she noticed Nate stiffen. She closed her eyes for a moment. That was one of those things she needed to work on. She was just so used to taking the lead on everything that she didn't always stop to think if she should. It might be her store they were working on, but this was Nate's project— he was the expert and he probably already had a plan in mind.

Yet here she was, taking over.

"Scratch that last bit," she said. "I just want to thank you all from the bottom of my heart and let you know that you're welcome to all the coffee, hot chocolate, and water you need. Nate is in charge, and he's going to let us know what to do."

And, of course, Nate had a plan, and immediately asked a few specific people to help him with pulling the tree away from the building and then cutting it up, then said his brother would lead a group to pull all the damaged parts of the building off and to clean up the bigger chunks of debris, then put Tory in charge of the group cleaning up the smaller rubble, like the bricks. She had mentioned to him that her kids were going to be coming to help— it was thoughtful that he put her over the thing that they would be able to best help with.

As Nate talked about where to put logs and tree branches, construction materials like wood and siding, bricks, and pieces of broken glass, Tory glanced around to see if she had somehow missed her kids being dropped off. She spotted Trace's car as it turned on to Main Street and pulled up near the crowd to her left. The doors opened and her kids hopped out, each holding their overnight bags. But Elodie got out without a jacket on.

"Excuse me," she whispered to Nate, and then she jumped down from the truck and ran toward Trace's car as he was backing up to turn around. She waved her arms to get his attention, and he stopped and rolled down his window.

"Elodie forgot her jacket."

Trace shrugged. "Yeah, sorry. We were in a hurry to leave, and she couldn't find it."

"I told you we were going to be working outside, Trace, and it's a cold day." She let out a slow breath and then noticed something pink sticking up between the passenger's seat and the console. "Wait. Is that it?"

Trace leaned over and tugged on the sleeve cuff, and pulled the jacket from where it had been wedged into the small space. "Ha. I guess that's why we couldn't find it. All right, I've got to go." His eyes shifted for a moment to

Nate standing in his truck, and he added, "Isn't that the guy I saw at your house last night?"

"Yeah. He's the contractor."

Trace narrowed his eyes in Nate's direction. "He looks shifty."

Tory placed a hand on her hip and rolled her eyes. "He's not shifty. Don't you have clients to meet?"

Trace nodded, waved goodbye at their kids who all stood at the front of the car, and then finished backing up and drove away at speeds that could only mean he was trying to show off.

She turned to her kids, and as they walked toward the shop, she asked, "How was your night at Dad's?"

"It was awesome," Covey said. "He got a new game system, and we got to play on it all night long."

Aspen skipped alongside her. "We were having so much fun, so he let us stay up playing until eleven-thirty!"

They reached the fallen tree, and Covey and Aspen jumped over first, then Tory picked up Jackson and handed him to Covey while Elodie climbed over it.

"You seriously stayed up that late?" Tory asked Elodie and Jackson as she stepped over the tree. "All of you?"

Elodie put her hand in Tory's and they walked around to the back of the building. "I didn't think I could stay up that long because I was getting so tired at eight thirty like I always do. But then Dad said I could eat all the marshmallows I wanted and they were like magical stay-awake pills! Jackson didn't eat too many, so he fell asleep on the couch. We were having so much fun, though, that none of us even noticed when he did."

Tory rubbed a hand across her face and took a deep breath in and out.

"Did you bring breakfast, Mama?" Jackson said. "I'm a starvin' Marvin."

"You didn't eat breakfast?"

Tory looked to Covey, and Covey shrugged. "We kind of all slept in too long, and all we had time to do was throw our stuff into our bags and race out to the car."

And when they had such a busy day planned, too. Tory shook her head. They always came home resisting every rule that had always been one of their rules, but every once in a while, things went relatively normal at their dad's. She shouldn't have assumed that today would be one of those days. But she was a pro at dealing with these kinds of things now, so this was no big deal, she reminded herself.

She led them through the back door of Love a Latte, got them seated at the table furthest from the front of the building, and then got out four slices of the sandwiches she'd picked up from Joey's.

After getting them each a cup of milk and some napkins, she said, "When you're done eating, get ready and then come outside and find me. I'll show you what you can do to help. Covey and Aspen, will you please make sure that Jackson and Elodie are dressed—in the clothes in their bags, not pajamas— and that they have socks and shoes, and that all of you are wearing jackets and gloves?"

Both of her older kids nodded, and Aspen said, "We've got this, Mom."

Tory smiled at them, and then looked toward the plywood covering the front of her store. In one of the gaps between the sheets of wood and the damaged parts of the building, she could see a nice slice of Nate wrapping some ties around the trunk of the massive tree, and she just watched him for a good moment.

Yep. If she was anywhere near the ballpark— or even in the same city as the ballpark—of being ready to date again, Nate would be the one.

But she was so far from being mentally or emotionally able to date again that she couldn't even imagine it happening from where she was. She shook her head as she gave each of her kids a squeeze on the shoulder and headed out the back door.

six

NATE

Nate finished attaching the straps from the tree to the winch on the back of Beckett's truck, parked on the other side of Main Street, the straps going right over Snowdrift Springs in the middle, and then worked to clear everyone out of the way. Don Willards had already cut the part of the fallen tree that had been connected to the part that was still standing, so they were good to go.

If he'd have been smart, he would have pulled the tree away from the building before everyone arrived so he wouldn't have to worry about it hitting anyone. But the morning had been so busy that he hadn't been able to arrive early at all.

Things worked out more easily when his job was spent mostly as a project manager— making sure that the right equipment and the right building materials were at each site at the right time, and his crew and sub-contractors were all dispersed to the right project, all on a beautifully orchestrated timeline that would allow each home or building to progress as quickly as possible.

But he didn't have enough people on his crew, so just like a few previous years, he was spending a lot of time working alongside his crews and sometimes even doing the entire job of a sub-contractor when there was no other choice.

Once everything was ready and no one was in the way, he gave the signal to Beckett, and as the winch turned, the tree was slowly pulled away from the building. The winch made a high-pitched whining sound as the part on the right side of the building— the part that had hit first and had the biggest sections of the building fallen on it— stayed stubbornly under the debris. Then, with a final loud squeal, the tree broke free of the parts holding it down, and Beckett managed to get it pulled onto the road.

A cheer erupted from the crowd and Nate chuckled. Maybe it was a good thing that he wasn't able to arrive early and do this part before everyone came. It was a pretty awesome sight to see— he probably didn't show gratitude nearly enough for all the equally grand things he got to see on the job nearly every day.

"And we're ready to rumble!" he called out to the

crowd. "Team leaders, you've got about fifteen minutes before we fire up the chainsaws. Then for about thirty minutes, they'll be just about all you'll be able to hear, so if you need to get your team organized, now's the time."

He glanced over at Tory, who was gathering her team and giving instructions on where everyone should work. He was glad to see that her kids had made it out of the building in time to see the tree pulled free from the building. They seemed to like that.

He turned to his chainsaw-wielding team of three that included Don Anderson, Mike Carter, and his sister Jeigh, who looked more than a little excited to be on chainsaw duty. "I've got trimmers over here— let's get all the smaller branches cut off and out of the way first. Then we'll move onto the bigger branches, and then the trunk. We'll get everything cut first, and then we can worry about hauling them after, so we don't have to have the noise for too long. Don and Mike, why don't you take that end and Jeigh, you and I can work on this end."

The tree's branches seemed to be everywhere, all covered in leaves partway through their growing cycle. They started trimming off the branches on the side nearest the building so they wouldn't be covering the things that people needed to be hauling to the trailers, but there were so many bigger branches that it wasn't long before the clippers were no longer useful.

Once they all started up the chainsaws, he put in his ear plugs and focused on the tree, chopping off the big branches first and hefting them further out into the road and out of the way. Then, they tackled the trunk. With four people working on the massive thing at once, they each had to work to cut most of the way through, then as a group roll the log a bit to cut the part that had been underneath. Before long, they had developed a rhythm of cutting, rolling, cutting, shoving a log aside, and then repeating.

At one point, he had finished his cutting and while waiting for the last person to finish theirs before rolling, he glanced over at Tory. She was crouched down, picking up bricks and tossing them into the wheelbarrow with her team, which had included her four kids. Even the youngest one was picking up the bricks that were broken in two and hefting them into the wheelbarrow, looking like he was having fun doing it.

He had seen that there was a toy room in the back of Love a Latte— Tory could have easily told her kids to stay in there and play while the rest of them worked. He liked that she was having them help. It was exactly the kind of thing his parents had him and Jeigh and Beckett do when they were kids.

When the four of them finished cutting up the fallen trunk, they sawed the branches they'd cut free into more manageable-sized logs, and cut off the smaller branches they had missed before. By the time they had finished using the chainsaws, they were all breathing heavily and sweating. He and Jeigh both leaned against the front of his truck, recovering.

Beckett stopped what he was doing, grabbed three water bottles from the cooler filled with ice that Tory had a couple of teenagers haul out, and walked over to them.

"My arms are jelly," Jeigh said, eyeing the water bottle. "I'm not even sure I can hold that." But she reached out and took it anyway.

Nate's arms were feeling like jelly from the constant vibrating of the chainsaw, too, but he wasn't about to turn down the water. He guzzled his, and Beckett and Jeigh finished theirs just as quickly.

He needed a couple of minutes of rest before starting to load the logs into the back of his truck, and as he leaned against it, he found his gaze going to Tory. Now that the chainsaws weren't making so much noise, he could hear her oldest son beat-boxing along to the sound of the bricks being tossed into the wheelbarrow, the glass pieces being thrown into buckets, and parts of the building being pulled from the debris.

Every time the older of the two sisters tossed a brick into the wheelbarrow, she tapped a beat on the side of the wheelbarrow, adding to the music of the job. Everyone around him seemed to be working to that same beat, a bounce in their movements. It made him smile.

Jeigh nodded toward Tory. "You should just go over and ask her out already."

He jerked his gaze to his sister, and then he mentally growled at himself. Had he been that obvious?

"Oh, come on," she said. "It's time to get back on that horse again. You finished going to therapy and recovered from Eva a long time ago. It's time you started dating again."

He shook his head. "Not going to happen."

"Are you sure?" Jeigh asked. "Because I've noticed her making eyes at you whenever you weren't looking, too."

Surprise crossed his face too quickly to stop it, and he knew that Jeigh had seen it before he managed to put on a more neutral expression. "I decided that I was ready to date again with Bree, remember?" He had to try hard not to let his gaze shift to Tory. "It just isn't meant to work out for me, Jeigh."

Beckett shook his head. "That Bree was a real piece of work. She dumped him the second he wouldn't discount her remodel. And that after being married to someone as manipulative as Eva..."

"Oh," Jeigh said.

Hearing the doom of two very complicated relationships— his five-year marriage to Eva and his 4-

month relationship with Bree— still brought back a lot of painful memories.

Jeigh turned to him. "And now you're worried that if Tory shows any attraction toward you, it's because you're her contractor. I'm sorry, Nate. I didn't know."

Consciously, he hadn't been worried about that until Jeigh pointed it out. Bree was supposed to have been the relationship that would finally work out after so much time spent with a therapist to get over the damage Eva had caused. With as terribly as that had ended, it was likely that his subconscious already had figured that out, though, even if it hadn't clued him in on it yet.

Jeigh lifted a shoulder. "I just don't want to see you alone."

The truth was, he didn't want to be alone, either. He had just accepted long ago that "alone" as far as a spouse was concerned was what was in the cards for him. "I'm not alone. I have good friends, a good family, and I live in a good town."

"Oh, I know! There's a woman I work with in Mountain Springs who would be perfect for you. She lives not too far from me, so if you two started dating, you could stop by and see me every time you went out."

Nate stood up straight and threw his empty water bottle in the trash can near the cooler. "I'm feeling so rested now," he said. "Aren't you feeling rested, Beckett? We should get back to work— lots to do."

Jeigh gave him an exaggerated eye roll, but thankfully she stopped talking about his failed relationships and potential relationships and put her gloves back on.

Hard work. That's what he needed right now. Just good, honest, hard work. That's what would take his mind off Tory and a future lifetime of nights spent in front of the fire alone.

seven

TORY

Tory couldn't help herself from sneaking glances at Nate working. He didn't shy away from the toughest of jobs, and although he was the boss and could probably get away with a role of mostly directing all the work, he was working the hardest. And directing still. Even taking Trace's nonexistent work ethic out of the equation, if she compared Nate's work ethic to normal people's, it was still mind-blowingly impressive.

As much as she had admired him from afar when he came into Love a Latte for his weekly meetings with his foremen, she had never gotten a chance to witness the beauty of his muscles before today. He was picking up massive logs like they were bundles of feathers, and she could see his muscles straining the fabric of his t-shirt now that he'd ditched the flannel shirt.

Eventually, she noticed that she had been frozen, a broken branch in her hand, unmoving for who knows how long, just admiring the man. *Cheese and gravy, Tory*, she scolded herself. *Stop ogling your contractor*.

Her younger three kids were all on brick duty because the bricks were small enough for them to easily pick up and carry, even for Jackson. Covey, though, was helping her with some of the bigger debris that was in the same area. Quite a bit of it was various types of wood— flat pieces of broken plywood, two-by-fours that were nailed to other two-by-fours, window frames, trim— some was sheetrock, and most of it was attached to other pieces of debris. She and Covey were working together to get the pieces separated so they would lay flat in the trailer.

All of them seemed to be enjoying themselves, which usually wasn't the case when they were working hard. But it wasn't very often that the work they got to do was as unique as picking up pieces of a building, and they were actually smiling and sticking with it.

Which made her smile. It was important to Tory that she taught her kids how to work hard and enjoy it. There would always be work that needed doing their entire lives, and she didn't want them to ever shy away from it or feel like it was drudgery.

Her ex-husband had been a pro at playing, but work made him irritable and he yelled at the kids almost constantly when they were doing projects together. It always made her hopping mad, because she figured that was about the surest way to teach their kids to hate working. She wanted them to find the joy in it and hated that he always squashed that.

Tory pulled a section of used-to-be wall out of the wreck, a broken two-by-four nailed to another at a ninety-degree angle and laid one side down on the cement. She stood on top of it, and while she and Covey pushed on the part sticking up to pry the second board free of the first, she noticed that her kids had started a game with their chore.

"Boop, boop, boop," Jackson said, putting his brick up in the air with each "boop" as he walked it to the wheel barrow. After the first "boop," Aspen and Elodie did the same.

Once they all dropped their bricks and headed back and picked up another, Elodie said, "Shimmy, shimmy, shimmy," shaking her shoulders back and forth, and Aspen and Jackson mimicked the motions and words.

Once she and Covey got their two boards separated, Covey ran to throw the broken boards into the trailer as Aspen led the others with a "Chonk, chonk. Chonk, chonk," while tipping her brick side to side.

It was one of Covey's favorite work games, and he immediately ran to a spot where a board was sticking out from the debris, with the board it was nailed to still trapped underneath a section of the roof.

"All at the same time," he said, and to a chorus of *shimmy shimmies, boop boops*, and *chonk chonks*, he added to the mix the jarring *reeeeeaaaak!* of a nail getting pried free from wood. All the different sounds mixing were music to her ears. She never knew if it was because all the different beats just sounded great together, or if it was simply because it was the sound of her kids enjoying work.

Tory glanced over from where she hefted a piece of plywood covered in shingles and saw Nate headed from the trailer right to where her kids were working. He was probably upset that the kids were messing around when it was time to work. She nearly stepped in to let her kids know that maybe everyone else didn't appreciate the extra noises, but before she could, her kids saw Nate nearing and paused mid-beat, obviously assuming Nate would respond the same way their dad always did to this game.

Nate reached down and picked up a section of the store front where half a dozen bricks were still in one piece, their mortar still holding them together, and said, "Be-dum-dum-crash. Be-dum-dum-crash" as he tossed them into the wheel barrow.

All four kids grinned widely at Nate's unexpected reaction and immediately resumed their own rhythms. Tory smiled as, one by one, at least a dozen other people helping to clean up added their own sounds to the collective rhythm. She added hers, too, just like she did at home when her kids started this game.

At one point, she watched Nate as he and Beckett lifted a massive section of roof, straining under the weight of it and looking like some kind of Greek god. Between the grunts of lifting, he still repeated his part of the rhythm. He still kept the game going even when no one expected him to, and it made her heart melt like caramel on coffee.

She had heard that guys like Nate existed in the world, but she hadn't realized exactly how jaded and cynical her divorce had left her until she noticed how surprised she was at seeing Nate working so hard, yet still managing to be kind to her kids.

He must've felt her eyes on him because he looked in her direction. When their eyes met, he smiled at her. A smile that wasn't just a contractor smiling at the person who hired him, or at someone who might be passing another person on the street. This was a real smile, big enough that it even made his ears move. The kind you can't fake— the kind you can only give when you really are enjoying yourself.

His face was already tanned from the amount of time he'd spent outside on construction sites this season, the crinkle lines by his eyes showed, and he had dimples! How had she never noticed that before? They were like upside-down exclamation points to his smile that made her heart beat faster and faster.

She shook her head. *Seriously, Tory? Now you're ogling*

your contractor's smile? Could a smile be ogled? Because she was pretty sure she was ogling his smile.

But it was a really great smile. If she was looking to fall for a guy with a great smile, he would be it.

But I'm not looking, she reminded herself.

The weather warmed up a bit— just enough to keep everyone from getting cold while they worked. With so many people helping, they were through cleaning up just before noon, which was so much sooner than Tory had even imagined.

Just before the last few items were picked up and tossed into the trailer, she grabbed her kids and Cory and Kyle, a couple of teenagers who didn't look quite as exhausted as the others, and headed into Love a Latte through the back door. She didn't want people leaving before she could feed them and give them a hearty thank you.

Her two helpers carried out a second cooler of sodas and water bottles while she had her kids help clean all the coffee and hot chocolate cups and thermoses off the rolling cart. Then she and Covey put the giant sub sandwiches on the cart, while the other kids piled paper plates and napkins and individual bags of chips on the middle shelf.

Getting the cart out front was so much easier this time without the massive tree and parts of her building blocking the way.

Everyone must've worn themselves out pretty well based on how quickly the sandwiches started disappearing. She grabbed a couple of plates, and put some sandwiches on both along with a bag of chips on each, balancing them in one hand like she'd done hundreds of times over the years when she'd dished up her kids' plates. Then she grabbed a couple of water bottles with her free hand and took it all over to where Nate was hooking the trailer up to his truck.

He looked up from where he was crouched, messing with a lever at his trailer hitch, and saw the plates of food. "Ahh. Manna from heaven."

Tory ducked her head, feigning a shy smile. "Nate, I've told you that you can't call me that when we're in public."

He laughed and stood, accepting a plate of food and a bottle of water. They both set their water bottles on the side of the truck, then leaned against it and took a bite of their sandwiches.

"Holy guacamole," Tory mumbled around a bite. "Doesn't food taste so much better when you've been working hard?" Nate nodded, and she looked him up and down. "Food must taste really good to you every single day."

He might have blushed just a bit— it was hard to tell under that tanned skin. "That's why I majored in Construction Management. In my intro class to it in college, my professor said that this job came with near magical taste buds."

Tory swallowed. "Wait, seriously?"

Nate chuckled. "No. But he did promise that if we did it right, we wouldn't ever have to pay for a gym membership."

Tory took a bite to hide the smile that came with the thought that he was doing it exactly right.

As they ate, they looked out across the space that had been filled with broken pieces of Love a Latte just two hours earlier. New plywood still covered the front of the building and blocked any entrance from the street, but it looked about a million times better with all of the remains cleaned up. She noticed that someone had even managed to sweep the sidewalk while she'd been inside getting the sandwiches.

"Thank you," Tory said, "for all of this." She noticed as she gestured that her hand also motioned to the full truck and trailer. "Oh! We should probably help you get this unloaded. Do you want to do it now? Or should we wait until later?"

"I've got a job waiting on the trailer. As soon as we're finished here, I've got a couple of guys who are going to help me unload."

Tory's reached out and grabbed Nate's arm. "You still have to go to work today?" She was so exhausted that she figured she might have a movie-watching party with the kids when they got home instead of their usual Saturday afternoon clean-the-house party.

Nate nodded toward the sky. "There's still quite a bit of daylight left. We've got a lot of jobs that need work."

And here she was, making him work even more by taking on Love a Latte. She wished she had any other choice. "Well, clearly I should be doing more than just bringing you a sandwich."

Nate looked out over the area they had just cleaned up. "Clearly. This is the kind of thing that calls for homemade pie."

Tory hesitated a moment, then put her plate on the side of his truck near her water bottle and headed for her store. Her kids were all sitting in a little circle on the sidewalk next to Love a Latte with a few of the teenagers, eating their lunch. She raised an eyebrow and gave them a questioning two thumbs up, and they all responded with their thumbs up, letting her know they were good. So she headed around to the back of her building and went inside and to the front counter.

Yes! There were still a few cookies in the case. She pulled out a chocolate chip one and cut it on two sides so that it came to a point on one end, the other end still rounded. There. That kind of looked pie-shaped. She put it on a small paper plate and then opened the fridge and pulled out a can of sprayable whipped topping. She put a fancy swirl on top of the cookie like it was a piece of pumpkin pie and took it back out front.

Nate's plate was on the side of the truck near hers, but he had a sandwich in his hand and was eating it while he was checking that the back of the trailer was secured. She held the plate in both hands and walked up to him, a smile on her face.

"I brought you pie. Okay, admittedly it's not homemade. In fact, it was baked a few days ago, so it's probably a little stale. And although it's not actually pie, it's more or less *shaped* like pie."

Nate let out a booming laugh and then tipped his head in a little bow. "Because I have those magical taste buds, I'm sure it'll taste like pie."

"Magical taste buds have got to be more valuable than not paying for a gym membership. Your construction management teacher should've led with that."

"Moooom!"

She jerked around at the sound of one of her kids calling for her in a not-so-happy voice and saw Jackson get up from where he'd been sitting and head toward her, arms crossed, brow furrowed, stomping, while Aspen stayed sitting and gave an exaggerated innocent shrug like she couldn't possibly guess why Jackson was upset.

"Duty calls. But seriously, Nate, thank you."

NATE

Nate walked into the chapel and slid into the bench his family always sat on, where Beckett, Beckett's wife Kimberly, their two kids, and his parents had already taken a seat.

From the other end of the pew, his mom glanced up at the clock that showed one minute until the meeting started and quirked an eyebrow. She liked to give him grief about how he cut punctuality to the wire during construction season. He gave her the A-okay sign because he liked to remind her how arriving one minute before something started was better than arriving one minute after it started. She silently chuckled.

As the pastor got up to the pulpit, Nate leaned back in his seat. This was the one time of the week when he felt like he could just kick back and be calm and not worry about anything other than what was being said at the pulpit.

His not worrying about anything was interrupted when he noticed that the pew where Tory and her family usually sat was empty. Not that he'd been looking. He chatted with his clients quite a bit over the course of a project and often became friends with them. Tory was no different.

Yesterday, though, there was a moment when he'd realized that he had enjoyed chatting with her a little too much. Now was the time to pull back, not the time to notice if she wasn't at church.

Besides, she and her kids came in a few minutes late at least one out of every three Sundays, so there was no reason for him to even make note of the fact that she wasn't here yet. He focused back on the pastor for a full seven minutes before he glanced at the clock again. When she was late, she wasn't usually this late. Not that he typically noticed. Not any more so than he noticed any other family here.

His three-year-old niece, Chantele, made her way over to him, a baggie of Goldfish in one hand and a box of crayons in the other, a coloring book awkwardly tucked under her arm, and sat down on the bench next to him. Between paying attention to the meeting and to Chantele, Nate managed to not think about Tory at all until she and her kids came into the chapel. Tory mouthed *Sorry* to the pastor as she hurried her kids up the aisle and to their seats. Nate smiled and guessed that she hadn't yet noticed that her youngest was wearing one dress shoe and one gym shoe.

Or maybe she had noticed it right before they came in, but she figured that arriving— he glanced up at the clock — eleven minutes late was better than arriving twelve minutes late. As she got all of her kids seated, after a couple of them switched seats twice, he thought about how impressed he was that she got them there each week by herself. It couldn't be easy— he only had himself to get to services, and he managed to get there just one minute before it started.

As the pastor was talking about holding fast to your beliefs through life's challenges, he found his mind drifting to Eva. For their entire marriage, he had been trying to have children with her. But if they had stayed married and had kids, he couldn't picture her being okay with bringing even one child to church on her own— especially once they were mobile and it became a challenge to keep them seated. Eva's motto was "If anything worth doing is difficult, it's worth getting someone else to do it."

After the meeting finished, he helped Chantele put all the crayons back in the box, including the two that had fallen on the floor that he hadn't been able to reach during the services. As they worked, he asked her to tell him about the pictures she'd drawn at the bottom of one of the pages. It was a line of people, and each one was a head with a crooked smile, and each person's arms and legs were drawn coming directly out from their heads.

"This one is you and this one is Daddy. I drew you both the tallest because you're so tall. And this is Casey. He's holding Mommy's hand because a soccer ball hit him right in the stomach and it still kind of hurts. Oh. I forgot to draw his stomach." She drew an imaginary circle with her finger right below Casey's head. "Pretend there's a stomach there. And that's Grandma and Grandpa."

As Chantele told him more about her picture, he kept finding himself glancing in Tory's direction as she and her kids chatted with others while the congregation slowly made their way out of the chapel. It was like his eyes were magnetically drawn to her. He had to stop doing that. Sure, he had enjoyed working alongside her for hours yesterday and talking with her as they ate lunch. He had enjoyed it quite a bit, actually.

But his relationships never ended well. Ever. Not once in his life— even before Eva. He had been cursed to be attracted to the person who things were least likely to work out with. No, it was more like he had been cursed to be attracted to the person most likely to end in disaster and the highest number of casualties.

Besides, Tory had four kids. Sure, his greatest desire was to have kids, but hers weren't babies who would give a new dad a chance to figure things out as he went. They were already kids— all in elementary school, even— and he didn't know the first thing about being a dad.

It was better for both of them if he just squashed his feelings for her right from the start.

———

After services, it was a beautiful enough day outside that everyone gathered on the lawn for the after-church potluck picnic and to soak up the sunshine. As he was loading his plate with food, he started thinking about his projects and what needed to happen for each. The schedule for all of them was tight with the amount of manpower that he had, so planning down to the detail was something he'd learned was a lifesaver.

But before long, his thoughts had strayed from planning to worrying. After working with a therapist for two years to recover from his marriage to Eva, he finally learned that gratitude was the key to everything. That things like worry, fear, and doubt not only kept him from enjoying the moment, but they also stopped all progression and momentum dead in its tracks. After working for so long to make gratitude his go-to, he had gotten quick to recognize when the train had switched tracks and he needed to get it back on.

His long string of busy construction months used to end in a haze, like he was just coming out of a cave, squinting at the sun. It had always left him feeling like he had been in some other world for months and wasn't aware of what had been going on around him. He found that gratitude kept him in the moment, enjoying every day. Since he had started consciously showing more gratitude, construction season had stopped feeling like it was lost to the void each year.

So he went and talked with Gary Klein, who was recovering from knee surgery, and sent up a little zing of gratitude for his health. He chatted with a group of older women who made up the bulk of Helping Hands and sent up gratitude for the kind people who surrounded him. He soaked in the warm air and sunshine, and after the last week of rain and cold weather that had made working outside a challenge, he was extra grateful for the mild weather.

And as Tory broke away from the group of friends she was chatting with and headed his direction, looking amazing in that skirt and those heels, a smile lighting up her face, he thought about how grateful he was to already have the knowledge that things wouldn't work out between them, and for the determination he had to keep things between them purely professional.

"Doesn't this sunshine feel incredible?" she asked as she neared, closing her eyes and tilting her face toward the sun, a golden glow bathing her features.

"You can count me as a fan."

"How did unloading the trailers and truck go?" Tory asked.

"It went fast, actually." Did her eyes just flick to his arms? Was she checking out his muscles through his suit coat? He let his smile show— there was no harm in a friendly smile. "It just wasn't quite as much fun to unload without the beat your kids added to the mix. I really could've used them to keep my crew going on the house we were sheetrocking. We were keeling over left and right."

Tory laughed, and the sound was joyful and musical and reminded him to be careful. Business only.

"So what you're saying is that your dinner last night tasted like it was made by the top chef in the state."

"Definitely five stars."

There must have been something in his expression that changed because a look of confusion flashed across Tory's face briefly before it looked like she changed her mind about saying whatever she had planned to say.

After a small hesitation, she said, "I know that we have people coming once again to help tomorrow at six— if we didn't work them so hard yesterday that they're hobbling from sore muscles today and it scared them off. What time would you like me to be there? Is there anything we need to do beforehand?"

He shook his head. "Nope. The lumber is set to be delivered to the site tomorrow morning. We'll need to talk soon about whether you want to make any changes to the materials used on the exterior, but since you're keeping the dimensions the same as they were before, I was able to get the measurements yesterday and I've made the plans. We just need manpower to get the walls raised and to put up the plywood to cover it. Then I can come in the evenings after I finish up with my other sites."

There. He was keeping it professional. This was easy. He could keep this up. "If I could just get the keys to the shop so I don't have to bug you each time I need to work on it, that'd be helpful." And it would make it so they didn't have to have quite so many interactions. Perfect.

Tory reached into her purse, pulled a set of keys out, and placed them into his hand, her soft skin touching his and sending flames of attraction racing up his spine. He bounced the keys a couple of times, trying to act casual. "I'll head over there in a few minutes so I can measure and get some plans made for the inside."

Before he realized what was happening, Tory snatched the keys back out of his hand. "Absolutely not."

He blinked. Did he just offend her? Did she not want him inside Love a Latte when she wasn't there?"

"It's Sunday, Nate. Everyone— even thoughtful, service-minded contractors— needs a day a week when they can just chill and not go to work."

He reached for the keys. "Really, it's no big deal. I have

limited time to spend in the shop, so I need to take the moments I can."

Tory crossed her arms, the keys tucked away, hidden. "If it takes a little longer, it takes a little longer. I'm not going to repay your generosity by killing you off." She nodded in the direction of his parents and sister-in-law. "I happen to know that you have a family dinner tonight. Enjoy the beautiful day. Go do something you like to do. Spend it with family. Whatever. I'll give the keys to your mom, with strict instructions not to hand them over to you until after dinner. The shop can wait until tomorrow."

Then she walked away, leaving Nate standing there slack-jawed and wondering what just happened. When he was married to Eva, he never made enough money for her tastes, and he had learned quickly that playing or relaxing when there was money to be made just earned him heaps of disapproval.

When he'd finally started dating again, Bree was most affectionate when she wanted him to keep working on her remodel even after exhaustion hit. He was so used to being asked to constantly sacrifice.

To see someone who desperately needed to have her shop back actually turn away time spent working on it was something he hadn't expected at all. He watched as she walked over to a group of people, and when the toddler that Joselyn Williams was holding reached out for her, she took the little girl and immediately started making silly faces at her.

When he realized he had just been staring at Tory, marveling at her, he shook himself out of it and looked around. Maybe he could stay and enjoy the day a bit more. A Frisbee came flying in his direction, so he leaped up into the air and caught it, then with a flick of his wrist, sent it back in a beautiful arc to the boy who had thrown it.

nine

TORY

When Tory had first told Nate that she was going to sell coffee on the sidewalk in front of the shop, she'd been joking. But the more she had thought about it, the more sense it made. She knew that many of her customers thrived off that little bit of heaven that her drink choices brought them each morning. And if she could provide them with something that made their days start a little brighter, she was all for it.

Besides, the weather cooperated beautifully. The mornings were still a bit chilly, but as soon as the sun was up, the days were pretty glorious. She had set up an eight-foot square easy-up awning, two long folding tables, a cash belt and her portable credit card reader, and brought out a cart filled with insulated coffee pitchers, creams, sugars, caramel, spices, and a cooler with cream and milk.

It was nice to be outside smelling the fresh air and seeing all the people that she had grown to love seeing each morning. Plus, she didn't want any of them to get in the habit of going somewhere else during rebuilding, and she didn't want to leave her employees without a source of income.

Nate had even been one of her customers early that morning when he had noticed that she was open for business. There had been plenty of times he'd come into her shop over the past year, and she had always checked him out, and, okay, possibly daydreamed about him a bit. But he let her pick his drink again, and this time when he came in, it was the first time that she'd helped a customer who had made her stomach flutter.

So apparently she had moved beyond "admire him from a distance" to having moments when she wondered if something between them could actually happen.

She'd given him an Americano. He'd looked like he needed it. She hoped it had given him a boost for the busy day he had scheduled. And, if she was admitting things to herself, she kind of hoped that the smile she had given him did the same. Maybe she'd find out tonight.

Business was at its afternoon slow-down right before it picked up again, so once she saw through the windows that Ruth and Katie had arrived through the back door and started preparing a cart of fresh coffees inside, she started packing up her cart.

When she finished, she took a moment to look up at her building. As great as it had been to get all the debris cleared away last Saturday, it was nothing compared to how fun it was to experience the change Monday night. About a half dozen people had shown up to help, and along with her kids, Tory had fed them all pizza, with help from Joey's Pizza and Subs.

Then they had gotten to work removing all the plywood that Nate and Beckett had nailed up the day of the storm, and went to work building the framework for her building. Nate was impressive. He worked so quickly and efficiently and directed all of them well— even though all but one of them had never done anything like it before.

He had even taken the time to explain to Aspen every little detail. Her oldest daughter had always been interested in crafty things, but Tory hadn't anticipated how much building construction would fascinate the girl.

Tory's favorite part was how quickly everything took shape, especially once they put the plywood up on the outside of the new framing. Nate had warned her that people always watched the speed at which their house would take shape during the framing stage and figured that it would all go that quickly, but it was all the less visible things that took the most time.

Still, though, there had been visible progress since Monday, and she hadn't gotten tired of gazing at the new front of her building yet. That night, they had nailed plywood over the window and door openings to keep her building safe, but the windows and door had been delivered a few days later, and Nate had installed them last night.

And they were usable. After the insurance adjustor had come, she had feared that her building would sit, half destroyed, for months. Yet just over a week later, she was pushing her cart through the front door, reveling in the fact that she no longer had to push it through the alley and around to the back of the building each time. They couldn't let customers in until enough of the rebuilding was finished that the building safety inspector would okay it, but the door sure was helpful to her and her employees.

"Hi, girls," she said as she rolled her cart toward the counter.

"Hi, Tory," Ruth said. "We are just about ready to go out."

As Ruth finished putting the items on their cart, Tory handed off the cash belt and the credit card reader to Katie. Then she gave last-minute instructions, said goodbye, grabbed her things, and hurried out of the store before climbing in her van and driving to the elementary school.

Since Trace had brought the kids back earlier than normal last Saturday, she'd managed to talk him into picking them up earlier today than his normal Friday pick-up time. That way she could head to her mom's sooner and still make it back in time to help Nate with the electrical wiring.

Even though Trace had brought the kids back unexpectedly early, she was still surprised that he so easily agreed to come to get them early this afternoon. She chuckled. He probably wanted to see if the contractor was going to be hanging out at her house again. If only Trace knew how often conversations between her and Nate had been strictly businesslike all week, he probably would've realized that Nate had zero interest in her and he likely would've said no about picking the kids up early.

When all four kids piled into the van, dropping their backpacks on the floor and jockeying for seats before getting their seatbelts on, Tory said, "I'm pushing pause in three, two, one, and pause."

Once they all quieted, she said, "Remember that Dad is coming to pick you up early. So when we get home, you'll have to grab a snack quickly, pack your overnight bag, and get your animals fed lightning quick. Give me thumbs up if you understand." She got four thumbs up, so she said, "And... unpause!" Then she listened as all four kids tried to talk over one another to tell her about their day.

By the time Trace arrived, visibly disappointed that his suspicions about Nate weren't confirmed and all the kids were finally in his car— after four times of one of them getting back out to run inside to grab something they'd forgotten— Tory collapsed into her van. She didn't know if her usual Friday post-send-kids-off exhaustion was because getting the kids ready to go with their dad was always chaotic, or if it was because her body knew that an eighteen-hour break from parenting was coming and it just needed to hold out until then.

Either way, being able to just sit for the hour-long drive to her mom's house was always a godsend.

Except it gave her a full hour to think about Nate. And to wonder why he'd gone from being friendly— and even a little flirty— one moment, to suddenly being nothing more than a contractor interested only in getting the job done the next.

Maybe the difference in his actions came every time he remembered that she had several kids running around, usually being some kind of crazy. He seemed to like children just fine, but just because someone liked being around a kid now and then didn't mean they were okay with the thought of stepping into a situation where they would instantly become a dad of four kids.

And that was okay. Yes, she'd had a bit of a crush on Nate for more-or-less the entire last year. And yes, it had somehow changed into something more when that tree fell on her building.

But both in the past year and right now, she wasn't looking to have a man in her life. She couldn't just introduce someone into her kids' lives and have them get attached. If things didn't work out, then they'd have to deal with him no longer being in their lives. They had already gone through that with their dad— they didn't need to go through anything resembling that ever again.

As she drove, though, she kept finding her thoughts coming back around to Nate and how thoughtful he was. And how quickly a smile came to his face, even when he was tired. Every morning she found more things finished in her shop, even though he must've been so tired by the time he got to Love a Latte each night.

And she thought about how she'd stopped by the shop on her way home from the grocery store on Thursday evening when she'd seen his truck parked out front. He'd had the headlights aimed at the building to give extra light as he installed the front door. She'd asked if he needed help, but he'd said he didn't.

When she had walked through the doorframe to see it from the inside, she'd bumped against the frame and some wood shavings had fallen onto her shoulder from where he'd drilled a hole for a screw. Nate had reached out and brushed the dust off, and butterflies had swirled around in her stomach, the likes of which she hadn't felt in more years than she could remember.

They were swirling in her stomach right now, just thinking about it again. If she had been looking for a man, she wouldn't look any further than Nate. It was too bad the timing wasn't better.

When she walked into her mom's house, she was surprised to see muddy footprints all over the entry way with some of it smeared, like a poor attempt was made at cleaning it. "Mom?" she said as she walked into the kitchen. "What is all this mud from?"

"Hey, Tory," she said, closing the notebook she was writing in. "Oh, a group of girl scouts came and planted flowers in my beds a couple of days ago. I invited them in for cookies after. Some didn't think to take off their shoes."

Tory sat down at the table next to her mom. "But doesn't the housekeeper I scheduled for you come on Thursdays? Did she not show up?"

"No, she did." Her mom got up and hobbled to the cupboard, the big air cast boot that protected her broken ankle banging on the tile, and got out a glass.

"Mom? What aren't you telling me?"

She pushed the glass into the water dispenser on the fridge door then turned and set it on the counter, not meeting Tory's eyes. "She's just been coming by less and less. She said now that my sling's off, I can do more and I need to quit being lazy and making messes."

She picked up the glass like she was going to take a drink, but just set it back down with a sigh. "When she saw the mud, she said she was there to clean up after one person— me. Not half the town. And she's right. I *should* have asked the girls to take off their shoes on the porch and since I didn't, I was agreeing to clean up their mess. But I tried, Tory. I just—" She motioned in defeat at the brace on her broken arm and the boot on her foot.

The more she talked, the angrier Tory got. Her mom was not a messy person, and the housekeeping was light. Her mom had injuries that couldn't be seen, too, like cracked ribs and a bruised spleen. "She seriously said those things to you?"

The mother that Tory knew was strong. Someone you didn't want to cross. Tory had seen her weak exactly twice. Once for about four months after her husband, Tory's dad, died, and now over the past four weeks since her car wreck. Even her voice and the words she was choosing were off.

That this housekeeper— someone who Tory had hired and had entrusted to help take care of her mom's home when neither she nor Christene could be there— had belittled her so much in her physically weakened state that she was now holding her head in shame made Tory's blood boil.

She felt the mama bear inside her that usually only emerged whenever her kids had been bullied rise up, and she picked up the phone.

"Tory, don't. It's okay. It's not that big of a deal."

The fact that her mom was backing down so easily from someone who had been working for weeks to demean her showed that it was a huge deal. Tory's heart pounded and heat rushed through her body.

When the housekeeping company answered the phone, Tory demanded to speak to the owner, and that it didn't matter that it was the end of the day on a Friday. She needed to speak with him *now*. She ground her teeth as she was waiting, pacing across her mom's kitchen. When they finally got the call connected, she gave him an earful about his employee that had been assigned to her mom and didn't hold back one tiny bit.

As she was talking on the phone, Tory noticed that her mom slowly began to stand a little taller and her shoulders went from being curled inward to being held back. She had gone from a shell of herself to looking so much closer to the mom that she knew. Not to the point she was at before the wreck, but pretty close to as tall and erect as a fifty-eight-year-old woman wearing a giant boot and an arm brace that went nearly to her shoulder could.

At the end of the call, Tory let the man know that they no longer needed his company's services. Then she jabbed her finger onto the icon to hang up the phone and set it on the table triumphantly, feeling much lighter. "I'll find you a new housekeeping company, Mom. One with great references, and I'll meet with them in person before they ever step foot in your house."

"You know," her mom said as she walked back to the table and sat in the chair across from Tory, "if you didn't attack every problem so fiercely, men might not find you so intimidating. One might even ask you out."

Tory sat down in the chair and leaned back, shaking her head. One phone call, a few minutes of some very firm words, was all it took and her mom was back to being herself. "You," she said, pointing at her mom, "raised me to be a fighter. A force to be reckoned with. So don't give me grief when I fight for something important."

For a brief moment, she wondered if her mom was right and that was the reason why Nate kept going from seeming at least interested in getting to know each other more to not interested at all.

But taking charge and standing up for what she believed in was who she was. Being a fighter was what had gotten her through all the tough things life had thrown at her, and she wasn't about to stop being that way just to please someone else.

ten

NATE

Nate couldn't exactly have the noise of a generator right in the middle of Main Street, so he was glad that the owner of the hair salon next door had agreed to let him plug an extension cord into her building. Nate ran the cord across the alley and in through the front door of Love a Latte, then plugged it into his work light. After several trips back out to his truck, he had all the coils of electrical wire and tools he needed.

Before he shut off the power to the building and lost the better lighting, he got all the prep work done that he possibly could, like laying out the wiring and getting each electrical box to the general location of where it would go.

He glanced down at his watch. Tory said she was going to be by at 6:30 to help, so she could be there at any minute. She had stopped by several other times this week, too. At first, it had annoyed him, because he had been trying hard to not be attracted to this woman and it was so much easier if she kept her distance, but he found himself looking forward to her arrival tonight.

He had just gotten the last of the wiring laid out that he would need for the wall plugs when Tory came in through the back door. "Sorry. I had hoped to get here sooner, but I couldn't leave my mom's house as early as I had planned. How's it coming?"

"Well, I haven't gotten to the hard part yet, so I'd say things are going pretty well."

She smiled at him, and it took his breath away.

He set the last electrical box near the wall where it would go, then walked over and turned on his work light. "I can see you wanting to help with the work when the manpower was all volunteers, but you're paying me for my work, Tory. There's nowhere in the contract that says you need to come help."

"And you're donating practically every bit of your time that isn't working or sleeping to do this job. Helping is the least I could do."

He tried to think of any other time in his career when a client stopped by to help with something not in the contract instead of just checking on the progress, and he came up blank.

He walked back to the storeroom where he had found

the electrical panel and shut off the power to the building so he could begin work. Then he felt his way through the darkened hall back to the employee door that led to the front of the store where his work light shone.

Unlike framing, doing the electrical work was a job he could do himself. But it sure was handy to have someone there helping him. After drilling holes in the middle of the two-by-fours in the framework, Tory helped guide the wiring through the holes from where one wall outlet would be to the next. He usually nailed the electrical box to the upright board first so it wouldn't move while he worked in the small space to get the wires threaded through it. But it definitely was easier having Tory hold the box steady near the wall while he more easily got the wires in the right place.

As soon as she crouched down next to him, her faint smell of something fruity— sun-warmed blackberries and vanilla, he decided— reached him and caused a fire in his chest to flame to life, and the fire seemed to be fed by her nearness. It had been a very long time since he'd last felt anything like it.

When they finished with one outlet, they moved on to the next, the two of them side by side, their shoulders or knees bumping, their hands frequently touching as they worked, her hands cool and soft against his warmer and coarser hands.

"How do you know how to do everything?" Tory asked,

a sense of wonder in her voice that sent a thrill through him.

He shrugged. "My parents built the house I grew up in. We moved in when I was five— the same day that the building inspector declared the house safe, even though the only semi-finished rooms were the kitchen, bathroom, and family room.

We set up the beds for all five of us in the family room, and then my parents finished the house room by room whenever they weren't at Elsmore Market. So I grew up watching and helping with the construction, fully believing that doing construction work was just as normal a part of growing up as making beds and cleaning bathrooms was to most kids.

"Then of course there was college, where the construction management course included classes for each sub-contracting aspect. Beyond that, it was just a matter of there always being opportunities to do it. Especially electrical work, so I make sure I maintain licensing for that outside of my contractor's license. I'm not as fast as my subcontractors are, since they specialize in one area, but it has come in handy over the years."

He glanced at Tory just then, and when he saw the look of admiration on her face, his arm muscles involuntarily flexed, like they were trying to get in on the showing-off action. He hoped she hadn't noticed. But a part of him kind of hoped that she had.

Tory pulled her phone out of her pocket and looked at the screen for a moment before she said, "Brooke said she's working late and noticed that we were here. She's heading to Back Porch Grill to pick up some dinner and wants to know if she should get something for us, too. Have you eaten yet?"

He shook his head. The truth was he was starving and pretty soon the growling from his stomach was going to be loud enough for Tory to hear.

She typed something into her phone and after a moment said, "She wants to know if there's something specific she should get, or if she should surprise us."

"Magical taste buds, remember? She could bring anything and I'd be happy."

They got back to work on running the wiring to the last outlet. After a moment of silence, he asked, "Do your kids enjoy going to their dad's?"

"They love it." Tory picked up the electrical box and held it out for him. "He's the fun parent, so it's always a party going there."

"Huh. After seeing the way you are with your kids, I would've guessed you were the fun parent."

She chuckled. "I'm the *responsible* fun parent, which is much less exciting than the *irresponsible* fun parent."

As he threaded the wiring through, her shoulder rubbed up against his and he suddenly needed to know why she wasn't with her ex anymore. If it was because of the same reasons why he and Eva or he and Bree had broken up, he needed to do something to stop being attracted to this woman right now.

He glanced down at her ring finger. She had kids and he knew that they were at their dad's house currently, but the ghost of an indent from years of wearing a wedding ring confirmed that she was married before. He paused, wondering how to bring up the subject. "Is that why you two divorced?"

Okay, that was blunt. But he needed to know.

Tory took a long, slow breath like she was trying to decide how much to tell or how to tell it. "In a nutshell." She shrugged. "It's funny because his playfulness was what originally attracted me to him. And when we were dating, engaged, and first married, it was great. We were still in college when we got married, and we did so many fun things together that I'd never been exposed to.

"It wasn't until he had lost his third job in the first six months after we graduated from college, which also happened to be the first six months that we were parents, that I clued in that he was only about the play and never about the work."

"You started having kids that quick out of college, then?" Here he was, quite a few years out of college, and he still didn't have a clue how to be a parent. Right then, he was a little bit jealous of her ex.

Tory let out a single breath of a laugh. "It wasn't the plan. We had gotten married super young, so we had decided to wait four or five years. But life has a funny sense of humor. So, yeah, right out of college. Covey was born twelve hours after I finished my last final in my last class."

He finished threading the wires and Tory passed off the electrical box to him to nail to the two-by-four.

"The new plan was to wait four or five years to have child number two. So of course I found out I was pregnant with Aspen when Covey was four months old."

Nate didn't know why— probably because his life during the same timeframe had been so starkly different from hers— but it made him laugh loudly. From her spot crouched next to him, Tory chuckled, then bumped her hip into his, knocking him off balance and onto the floor. He sat on the floor, his arms holding him up in a reclined position, a hammer still in one hand, and smiled up at Tory as she stood. "It seems that life didn't go quite as either of us had planned."

Tory opened her mouth like she was about to say something, then her eyes shifted to the door. Nate twisted to see Brooke open the door and come inside holding a bag of food. He jumped to his feet.

"I don't know what you brought us, Brooke," Tory said, "but it smells divine."

"My mouth's been watering all the way here. You're lucky I didn't stop on the way and crack one of these containers open to take a bite."

"What is it?" Nate asked.

Brooke lifted a single shoulder in a shrug. "Cole just said it was a pasta dish he was trying out."

"A pasta dish from the gods," Tory said.

Brooke brought the bag up to her face and breathed in deeply, bliss on her face. "And I get to marry the man who can do this to food."

"Would you like to join us?" Nate asked her.

Brooke looked between him and Tory like she was trying to decide if anything was going on between the two of them. He didn't know what exactly she was interpreting from what she saw, but after a pause, she shook her head no. "I better take mine back to Best Dressed to eat it. I can tell by the smell that I'm going to be moaning so much eating it that it'll be embarrassing." She put their two containers on one of the tables and said goodbye.

Nate headed into the restroom to wash his hands, while Tory washed hers at the sink behind the counter. When he came back out, he saw that she had set two drinks on a table and was laying napkins and plastic forks next to each food container.

As they ate, he kept asking Tory more about her marriage. From what he gathered, the guy she was married to, Trace, had been a real tool. He had gotten a great job right out of college, but he had lost it within two months. Tory had paid for college with scholarships and a lot of hard work, but Trace had piles of student debt, so she went to work part-time when Covey was just four weeks old.

He marveled at how loyal Tory had been in sticking by his side through it all. Eva, Bree, and virtually every woman he had dated before them would've called it quits years before Tory did. She just kept encouraging him and trying to make things work.

That was what had brought them to Nestled Hollow, actually, around the same time he had left. They knew they needed a better place to raise their kids and had been searching. When they came to Nestled Hollow, Tory had thought that the more relaxed atmosphere might be better for Trace, and when they saw this building for rent and the town's lack of an actual coffee shop, they figured it was the perfect business. They could run it together, so Trace wouldn't be pressured to please a boss, and they could be open in the mornings and be home with their kids after school.

But of course, it didn't take long before the guy was messing up even the most perfect of situations. It sounded like he found someone seven years younger who wouldn't make him pull his weight, so he left them. A wife and four kids, and he just left. Right between Thanksgiving and Christmas. Nate might not know a thing about parenting, but he knew enough to never do that.

Tory somehow told the story without bashing her ex, but Nate was bashing him in his head enough for both of them. He knew enough about getting divorced to know that each ex-spouse told a very different side of the same events, but still, he couldn't believe that someone would be stupid enough to throw away a life with someone like Tory.

"So, are he and the twenty-three-year-old married now?" Nate asked.

"Not yet, but I think they're getting close."

Tory stood. "Holy frijoles, I can't believe I just told you my life story." She ran her fingers through her hair, then picked up their empty containers, forks, and napkins, and took them to a trash can. She turned back to face him, looking flustered. "That's so embarrassing. I apologize."

"Don't apologize," Nate said, carrying their empty cups to the counter. "I enjoyed hearing it. Someday I'll tell you mine, and you'll realize that if either of us should be embarrassed, it's me."

She held out her arm and said, "Let's arm shake on it." He looked at her arm in confusion. "Come on, reach out and grab my arm up here by my elbow and shake, thereby committing you to tell me your story. It's something my kids do if they want to bind you to your word. Kind of like a pinkie promise or spitting in your palm and shaking hands, only since it's more of your arm, it's stronger. And less gross. Which is impressive, given my kids' tolerance for gross things."

He reached out, grabbed hold of her arm, and shook.

"Now," she said, "let's get going on the ceiling wiring before we both hit the post-pasta crash."

Nate set up his ladder and drilled the holes for the electrical wiring in the ceiling joists while Tory held the ladder from tumbling over every time he had to push too hard on the drill. The high-pitched whirring *rizzzz* of the drill sounded as he made another hole and then moved his ladder to the next joist.

He threaded the wire through the holes he had drilled, mounted the electrical box, and connected the wiring to the first and last of three lights. Connecting the wires from both directions to the middle light was proving to be rather problematic, though. It was too close to the existing ceiling sheetrock, so he couldn't nail the box to the joist to hold it in place and still have room to get his hands behind it to get the wires through it.

But he couldn't hold the un-mounted electrical box and still be able to connect the wires coming from both directions in such a small space.

"Here, let me hold the box while you do the wires," Tory said as she grabbed a step stool from behind the counter and set it up next to him. She stood on the top step, but she wasn't nearly tall enough to reach it.

"Switch me; I'm taller."

He climbed down from the ladder and Tory climbed up and reached high with both hands to grab hold of the box and the wiring on the side furthest from him. Standing on the shorter step stool, Nate had to reach up as high as he could to get both of the wires. Tory continued to hold the one on her side.

It was still tricky, though, especially doing it while reaching up so high, both of their necks craned backwards to see what they were doing, squinting in the light of the work light, which wasn't positioned as well as it needed to be for this one.

He finally got one set of wires twisted together and a cap screwed onto the bare wires, then the other set, and all of it pushed into the backside of the box.

Both he and Tory let out a simultaneous sigh of relief and their gazes dropped from staring up at the box to looking at each other. He hadn't realized that they were so close, standing nearly chest to chest, their faces inches apart. Heat crawled up his face. He cleared his throat and dropped his hand to rub the back of his neck. A blush covered Tory's cheeks.

"Well, that was...close."

Tory ducked her chin and climbed down the ladder, and Nate stepped off his stool.

"I, um," she looked left and then right, and then her

eyes landed on a roll of electrical wire. "I'll just start cleaning up while you nail that last box into place."

Nate chuckled softly as he climbed up the ladder and finished attaching the last electrical box, happy to see that their closeness had affected her in the same way it had him.

eleven

TORY

Tory's Saturday afternoons were almost always the same. After her kids came home from Trace's house all hopped up on playing games and eating junk food for hours on end, she attempted to undo some of the damage by feeding them a healthy lunch and then cleaning the house together. After a crazy week of work and school and homework and lessons and school projects and community events and sports, the house was always in sore need of a good cleaning by the time Saturday rolled around.

She did everything she could to make cleaning fun, to show them that it wasn't only playing that was fun, and that work also came with the bonus of the sense of satisfaction from seeing what you had accomplished.

At least that was her goal. Sometimes she succeeded;

sometimes she fell flat on her face. Sometimes the kids were too tired or too sluggish from an excessive intake of sugar to get much done without getting irrationally irritable. On days like that, it took a few days for them to fully get back into obeying the house rules that they had all the time but they never seemed to think they had to obey after they got back from their dad's.

But many times the plan worked beautifully and she felt like she was doing things right. She hoped that today was one of those days because after last week had been spent cleaning up the wreckage of the shop and fallen tree, the house was in pretty sorry shape.

So she pulled out the big guns: the mission cards. She had made sixty-two cards with a "secret mission" logo on the top, and each one had a mission to accomplish that was a small cleaning task. She put all the mission cards in a bucket and then named her kids Spies of the Royal Beckstead Family. Each kid had to pull a mission out of the bucket, do the task, and then turn in the mission card before grabbing the next card, and they had to complete the same number of cards as how many years old they were.

To keep it fun, they raced to see who finished first.

And to keep it even more fun, she was in the race, too, with her own set of thirty-two cards filled with small chores, since that's how old she was. Her kids seemed to think it was hilarious to see her racing around trying to get her chores done faster than them.

"On your mark, get set, go!" she called out before turning on her spy music soundtrack and blasting it through the house.

This was one of the more chaotic of their Saturday games, but it was the surest way to get a messy house cleaned quickly.

Each kid shouted out what chore number they were on each time they grabbed a new card, so they all knew if they needed to hurry more quickly to win. Today they all seemed determined to take home the prize.

Jackson had one card left, Elodie three, the older kids each had two, and Tory was racing to finish her last five when she thought she heard something. "Was that knocking?" she called out. No one answered, so she hurried to her music player and turned it down, cocking an ear toward the door. She heard a second knock, so she took off her rubber gloves and wiped a bit of sweat from her forehead with the back of her hand as she headed toward the door.

She opened the door, her hair in a ponytail, the hair at her temples probably curly from sweat, likely red-faced, and dressed in her too-worn sweats and a ratty t-shirt, to see Nate Elsmore standing at her door, dressed in jeans and a t-shirt and looking fine as ever, a stack of papers in his hand, mouth quirked up in an amused smile.

"Hi," she said.

"It sounds like Party Central here. And possibly evidence that you are, in fact, the fun parent."

"Want to come in? We do throw the best parties on the block." Last night had ended on an awkward note. So far today wasn't doing much to erase that.

Nate stepped into her living room, then Jackson came running into the room, panting. "First one done!" He saluted her and then held out five mission cards. "I'm ready for my debriefing, Ma'am."

Tory saluted back, took the cards, and gave him a high five. "Nice work, Secret Agent Jackson. Give me just a few minutes, and then I'll check these so you can choose your prize, okay?"

"Second place," Covey shouted as he skidded into the room, sliding across the hardwood floor in his socks and holding out ten mission cards in one hand and saluting her with the other. "I'm ready for my debriefing, too."

Tory took his stack of cards, too, and then returned the fist bump he held out. "Thanks, Covey. I'll come to check these in just a few minutes. Will you let everyone know that they can have thirty minutes of screen time as soon as they're finished?"

Covey ran to their family room, shouting that they all could have screen time as he went. Tory winced at the volume.

"I'm guessing I came at a bad time?" Nate asked.

Tory shook her head and led him into the kitchen. "No —coming *before* we cleaned would've been, well, a more embarrassing time at least. What's that you've got for me?"

Nate put the papers on the table and sat down in a chair next to Tory. "A list of decisions that need to be made for the shop. I've got some different choices for the exterior here, along with their prices and some pictures. There are also things like lighting, some paint, different trim choices, and flooring options."

Tory flipped through the packet. Page after page after page of choices that needed to be made. She took a slow, deep breath.

"It's a lot, I know, and it's always overwhelming. The decisions don't all have to be made at once, though. I'll start putting up the sheetrock Monday, so the paint will be the first decision I'll need. And I'm happy to answer any questions, or to give opinions on what kinds of things are most popular right now."

This all shouldn't be overwhelming. Maybe it was just because her heart rate still hadn't returned to normal after racing to get through her massive pile of cards before her kids. "I think I'll just take this with me to work on Monday, then, so I can be looking at the shop when I decide if that's okay."

Nate nodded, and she smiled at him. Sure, the evening had ended awkwardly last night, but she'd still come home practically floating. She'd had fun helping him, just the two of them, working in the glow of a four-foot-high work light. He was one of the most requested contractors around, and it was fun to see a small part of the reason why.

And it was extra fun to feel the spark that buzzed between them whenever they touched or brushed up against each other. Not to mention the spark between them that could've powered the entire room when she was on the ladder.

But as fun as it was, last night was just the two of them in a little bubble. Real life wasn't like that. Real life was like the chaos surrounding her.

"Done!" Aspen said, slapping her cards down on the table. "Although cleaning out the litter box should've counted for two cards this time." She made a retching sound and then did a full-body shiver to get her point across.

Nate smiled as Aspen skipped off to join the video game that Covey and Jackson were playing.

"I'm impressed. Your kids seem to understand the value of work."

There were so many times that she felt like she was failing as a mother. Too often, whenever she witnessed one of them not living up to their potential, she viewed it through the eyes of herself— of how she hadn't taught them all the things they needed to know. It was nice to step back for a moment and see them through Nate's eyes.

"Yeah, they are pretty great kids. I lucked out when I got to be their mom."

He flipped to the next section in the papers he'd brought. "Oh, and they don't make the tile you currently have anymore, so we won't be able to match it. I've listed some options of designs and tiles we can use that will go with what you have, and some options that will replace all the flooring in your lobby."

Elodie meandered into the room.

"You all finished, Sweetie?"

"Nope. I got the mission card for puzzles and got distracted by putting them together instead of putting them away. I remembered we were in a race, so I put them together really fast, though! I wish I would've had you time me." She reached into the bucket and pulled out a card, then pumped her fist. "Yes!"

Then she pulled out another and another— so she had only gotten through half of hers. She put all three face-up on the table. "I got *Feed the dog, Feed the chickens*, and *Feed the gerbil*. What are the chances?"

"You are one lucky girl," Tory said. And then, knowing how likely it was that Elodie would get distracted by something else before long, added, "How about I time you to see how quickly you can finish?"

Elodie shook her head. "I want Nate to come with me so I can introduce him to our pets. Can he?"

Normally, Tory would've given someone visiting her home a good excuse so they could say no without seeming rude. She would have said something along the lines of "Nate only has a few minutes, sweetie, because he's building some homes for people and probably needs to get back to it quickly." But she was a little too curious to see how he would react. So instead of offering an excuse for him, she just said, "I don't know. You'll have to ask Nate."

Elodie came around the table and stood right by Nate. "Do you want to come to meet our pets?"

"I would love to," he said, and then he even accepted her outstretched hand.

Tory walked with them but gave the two of them enough space so that Elodie didn't feel like she was encroaching on her tour.

Elodie led him to the kitchen pantry first. She opened the door, and then put the scoop into the bag. "You'll get to meet Nacho first. He gets a scoop of food right up to the top. You don't want to make it all piled up on here, or he'll get too fat to play. Then you just have to do this and he'll come running. Nacho!"

Sure enough, the dog came running as Elodie poured his food into the bowl, and she put her hand on his back and said that Nate could pet him, too. And he did.

Their cat, of course, ambled in, probably hoping she

could get some extra food and started rubbing up against Elodie. Elodie picked up the cat around its middle and held it out to Nate, claws first. "This is Cleopatrick. His name was Cleopatra at first, but then we found out he was a boy cat. You should hold him— he's super soft."

Tory put a hand over her mouth to hide her smile. Nate clearly wasn't a cat person, but he was a good sport about it and accepted Cleopatrick from Elodie's outstretched hands. He didn't even flinch too much when the cat clawed his way into a better position.

Since Nate's hands were busy with the cat, Elodie grabbed the corner of his shirt and pulled him toward the fish tank. "We don't have to feed these guys because it wasn't on my cards, but that's Petri Fish, Toaster, and Princess Flower Power House. That gold one in the corner is Cheese Boat, but we don't like him very much because he's kind of mean to the other ones. Oh. Where's Sneeko? Stick your head around this way— you can kind of see him hiding back here in the corner. He's a good hider."

Okay, so far Nate was doing better than most people that Elodie talked into joining her on the Tour of Pets. He was asking questions and not looking at all annoyed or in a hurry, even though Tory was sure he had a million things on his mental to-do list currently.

Then Elodie led him into the family room, around the backside of where her other kids were playing a video game that made them a little loud and crazy and introduced him to Marshmallow Chocolate Chip, their pet gerbil.

Cleopatrick didn't even jump out of Nate's arms until right about the time that Elodie led him out back to the chicken coop.

"Watch out," Elodie said as she opened the gate and let him inside, "there's poop practically everywhere over here, even though we clean it up a million times." Tory waited outside the fence, and Elodie shut the door. "That's Captain Jack and that's Applesauce and Tractor Tower over there. And this is Cherry Sprinkle Cakes. She's my favorite." Elodie picked up Cherry Sprinkle Cakes and cradled the chicken in her arms, rubbing her cheek up against the chicken's cheek. "I just love her *so* much. She lays the prettiest eggs, too."

Elodie got out the chicken scratch and spread it in the area where the chickens most liked to eat, and they immediately went to work pecking at it. Then she went to the coop and lifted the hatch before turning to grin at Nate. "You get a special treat because there are eggs waiting. Pull out your shirt."

Nate touched his fingers to the chest of his shirt, and said, "Pull out my shirt?"

Elodie rolled her eyes. "Not like that, silly. Pull out the front of it and hold it with both hands, like a basket. You'll need to untuck it."

Nate looked back at Tory, but she just gave him an

encouraging smile. You never knew what a kid was going to ask you to do. She wanted to know if that kind of thing threw him off.

It didn't. He pulled out his shirt and held it like a basket. Elodie started pulling the eggs out one by one and thanking each chicken who laid it. "Wow, Tractor Tower, you did it!" she said to their chicken who had struggled to lay eggs consistently. "Good job!"

Then she pulled out Cherry Sprinkle Cakes's egg and held it up toward Nate. "See what I mean? Isn't this the prettiest egg you've ever seen?" She pulled it close to her face. "It has all those little specks on it, and if you look close, it's like they're each a little bit different color. That's how you know that she laid it." Elodie called over to where the chickens pecked at their food. "Two thumbs up, Cherry Sprinkle Cakes!"

Watching the two of them together, she realized how easily Elodie could get attached to Nate, especially since she had been asking for a new dad. She also knew how devastated it could make her if things didn't work out. What was she doing even entertaining the thoughts of a relationship with Nate?

As they headed back to the house, Nate cradling the eggs in his shirt "basket," Jackson raced out of the house, video game controller in his hand, Aspen and Covey chasing after him, a raucous chaos of arguing and yelling.

"Whoa, whoa, whoa!" Tory said, putting her arm out

and catching Jackson as he raced past and pulling him to her. "What is going on?"

"Covey made me fall off a cliff and lose a life," Jackson said.

Covey came to a halt and huffed, "On *accident*. And I told him it was on accident, and he still got mad and shut it off right in the middle of a game and we didn't even save first."

"And I was about to win!" Aspen said, her hands on her hips.

Tory ran a hand over her face. She knew better than to let the kids play video games the day they got home from playing them for hours straight at their dad's. She had just taken the easy route to keep them busy while she talked to Nate, and obviously, that had been the wrong choice. "All of you, go in the house. Go find a space to cool down where you can be alone and not see each other. You've got five minutes, and then we'll talk."

Honestly, when the eruption happened, she expected Nate to mouth "I've got to go" and then slip off into the kitchen and grab his things while she made order of the chaos. But as Covey, Aspen, and Jackson stomped into the house, arms crossed, she looked over at Nate. He was standing there, still holding his shirt full of eggs, and he was *smiling*.

She cocked her head to the side, confused.

His grin just got wider. "They remind me of me, my brother, and my sister when we were kids."

Tory studied Nate for a few long minutes, then said, "Don't sheetrock Monday night. Go to the spring festival in the park."

He raised an eyebrow.

"We'd love to see you there." She paused a moment, then in a burst of bravery, she added, "*I* would love to see you there."

twelve

NATE

Nate sat around his parents' kitchen table Sunday night, laughing with his parents, brother, sister, sister-in-law, nephew, and niece, feeling lighter than he had in ages. Doing the electrical work at Love a Latte on Friday night had been unexpectedly enjoyable, and dropping in at Tory's house on Saturday had shown him a glimpse of her that he hadn't seen before and hadn't expected. It had been like a cool breeze through a construction site on a hot summer's day.

And much to his surprise, he could attribute much of his great mood to anticipating the spring festival tomorrow, which had caught him off guard. He hadn't gone to one of them in probably nine or ten years.

His nephew, Casey, sat in the chair next to him and grinned. "I like when you come to family dinners."

"Me, too, buddy. Me, too." Nate gave him a fist bump.

"Mommy says that you're coming to the park tomorrow," his niece, Chantele, said.

He nodded.

"And you're going to sing," Casey said.

"Ha ha. Funny. Good one, Case." Nate put a fork full of mashed potatoes into his mouth.

"But—" Casey flashed a confused look at his parents, causing Nate to nearly choke on his potatoes. He threw a look at his brother.

Beckett ducked his head and rubbed the back of his neck, trying to act remorseful when his face was filled with mischievous cheerfulness. "I'm so glad to see that you're in such a great mood, bro, because here's the thing. Remember how they were talking about the spring festival so much at the luncheon after church today? Well, Whitney Brennan was going around with a clipboard, trying to get some more people to sign up to do musical numbers at the festival and, well, I signed us up as 'Belt-it-out Builders.' I already texted Mark and Jens. The four of us are all going to be at the Rasmussen site tomorrow, so we can figure out what we're going to sing and practice while we work."

By the way everyone around the table was grinning, they all knew this already. He was never going to show up late to a family dinner again. "I am not going to go up there and make a fool of myself." Especially when Tory was watching. And her kids.

"It's not like you'll be there alone," Beckett said. "If we crash and burn, the embarrassment will be spread between the four of us, so we'll each only get a fourth of the way embarrassed."

Nate shook his head at how ridiculous it all sounded.

"You're not going to make fools of yourselves," his mom said. "Remember when you used to sing in the church choir and the high school choir?"

"I was a kid, Mom."

Beckett shrugged. "Mrs. Davenport has the guts to get up and sing every single year, even though she has to have a couple of guys carry her wheelchair up on stage. And she even sings a song she makes up on the spot. If she can do it, so can we."

"I think you should do it," Jeigh said. "I'll video it, so we can rewatch it and relive the joyous moment even when we're old and can't remember each other's names."

"Oh," Kimberly said, "and make sure you all wear your hard hats and tool belts so you live up to the name."

His dad cleared his throat. "You know, Son, if you're nervous because you're not sure what you should do while you're up there, I can choreograph something for you."

Nate's mind flew to the dance his dad did on Christmas morning when he opened one of his gifts and found an 8-in-one tool set that folded to the size of a pocketknife inside.

"Say yes! Say yes! Say yes!" Casey and Chantele chanted.

"You all are crazy."

"I'm going to take that as a yes," Beckett said.

Nate shook his head in defeat but then nodded. He was going to regret this. He was so very much going to regret this.

———

For a second, Nate thought maybe he wouldn't regret saying yes to singing. He, Beckett, Mark, and Jens had been singing on the job all day, and he had been enjoying it. They even had some dance moves down, and he kept picturing them up on the portable stage in the park, and a thrill went through him.

But now that he was stepping into Snowdrift Springs Park and seeing all the people everywhere, any excitement felt earlier in the day was replaced with nerves. He had hoped to leave the site early and arrive in the park by six because he knew that it got dark just a bit after eight, and it was a school night, so the festivities weren't bound to go on too late.

But right when he was leaving, a pipe in a bathroom had broken when one of his crew had pounded a nail into it from the other side of a wall, and it took longer than he had time for to fix it. He had texted Tory to let her know that he wouldn't be arriving until six-thirty and rushed home when they were finished to grab a quick shower before heading over.

He hauled the crate that held their tool belts and hard hats to just behind the curtain that formed the backdrop of the stage at the side of the open field and then headed off to find Tory.

Dozens of people milled around each of the activities, and it took him a bit to find Tory, especially with so many people stopping him to say hello. With as late as he was, they had probably already done most of the activities.

Eventually, though, he got to the part of the park where people were making crowns out of flowers. Tory, Aspen, Elodie, and Jackson were sitting down at a table, a pile of flowers and ribbons in front of them. Tory was wearing a casual, spring-like floral dress that looked so incredible on her that he thought this was probably why people did things like have spring festivals. Without meaning to, he found his eyes traveling to her bare legs that looked lean and smooth and made him realize just how much he needed to keep his eyes on her eyes.

Covey stood next to Tory and kept glancing at where some kids were racing aluminum foil boats down Snowdrift Springs. As Nate neared, Covey noticed him, crossed his arms, and stomped off toward the boat races. He wasn't earning points with the kid anytime soon.

Nate wove through the last few people and Tory smiled up at him and said, "Hi! I'm glad you could make it."

"Me too," Nate said, which was true if he didn't consider the part of the night where he'd be up on stage and only thought of this part, where he got to see Tory. He motioned toward Covey. "Did I do something?"

Tory shook her head. "He just wanted to go off with friends to race boats. Want to make a flower crown?"

Aspen was completely focused on her crown and seemed to be doing just fine on her own. Tory sat between Elodie and Jackson but was currently helping Elodie, so Nate sat down on the other side of Jackson. "Want some help, buddy?"

"Yes," Jackson said, dropping the wire he was trying to form into a circle. "I keep trying to get it to stay in a circle, and it just won't!"

Nate worked with his hands all day long— he could do this. He glanced at Tory and saw that she had taken the bendy wire and wrapped it around the crown of Elodie's head to get it the right size and then twisted the wire around itself to get it to hold into place, so he did the same with Jackson's.

"Aspen, do you want help measuring yours?" Tory asked.

Aspen's looked like it might be a little big, but she shook her head and said, "I've got it."

Nate had never made a flower crown before in his life, but Tory and her kids seemed to know what they were doing, so he watched them to see what to do. Jackson tore off a strip of floral tape and grabbed his first flower and held it to the wire. He seemed to want to do all the work himself but was struggling to hold the flower in place on the crown while trying to wrap the tape around the flower stem. So, as Jackson placed each flower, Nate held both it and the crown steady while Jackson wrapped the tape.

Jackson forgot to pull the tape tightly in several places so some of the flowers were a little loose, but the kid seemed so proud of the work he was doing that Nate didn't step in to help. It was nice, just sitting at a town event, chatting with Tory and her kids. It felt like it did when he hung out with Beckett and Kimberly and their children. He had wished for moments like this for himself plenty of times when he was married to Eva, but a part of him must have known that it would never happen because it was never as real in his head as this moment was.

Maybe a family was something he could actually have. Maybe he wasn't destined to live and die alone.

A few measures of a song sounded through the speakers before Mayor Stone said into the mic, "Testing, testing."

"Momma," Elodie said, "we have to hurry! The music festival is about to start!"

Nerves fluttered in Nate's stomach. He had sung in the congregation at church plenty of times. On job sites, too. But it had been nearly fifteen years since his senior year of high school when he had last sung in front of a group of people.

The mayor introduced the first singer, and a high school girl with a beautiful voice sang, prompting dozens of families to lay their blankets on the grass in front of the portable stage and watch. Nate, Jackson, Tory, and Aspen all raced to finish their crowns.

"Done!" Jackson said triumphantly, holding his crown out for all of them to see. Then he shoved it down on his head and climbed onto his chair and stood, arms crossed, looking proud as could be to be wearing the crown he'd made.

Aspen and Elodie finished theirs not long after. Aspen came around to Nate's side of the table and held out hers. "This is for you."

"For me?" he said, bewildered. "You don't want to keep it?"

"Nope. I made it for you." Her grin was spread across her face.

Nate glanced at Tory, but she just smiled at the two of them. So Nate said, "Thank you. I am honored to wear it," and bent down so Aspen could put it on his head. She had overestimated the size of his head, so it was a little big and kept falling down onto his neck.

The last few notes sounded of a country song a man was singing, and applause came from the field. Nate glanced toward the stage as a few guys lifted Mrs. Davenport's wheelchair onto the stage, and the old woman wheeled herself to the microphone. Nate turned back to Aspen. "I've got to go do something for just a minute. Can I take this with me?"

She smiled and nodded, seeming pleased.

Tory looked like she wanted to ask where he was going, but held back. Instead, she said, "We are going to head over to the field to watch the music."

Nate nodded. "I'll look for you in just a few minutes." Then he hurried off to meet up with Beckett and the others. He didn't know why he didn't just tell Tory where he was going. He realized that it wasn't completely because he wanted to surprise her by getting up on stage. There was a small part of him that was afraid still.

Eva hated small towns and had made it abundantly clear that she would never live in Nestled Hollow or a town like it. But if he somehow would have been there with her instead and had decided that he was going to get up on stage and sing, she would've been so embarrassed that she would've left the park entirely before the first note sounded over the speakers.

Beckett, Mark, and Jens were already behind the stage,

the curtain blocking them from the view of the crowd, putting on their tool belts and hard hats. Nate did the same and placed the too-big crown of flowers on his hard hat as Mrs. Davenport sang the song she was making up as she went along.

"Nice touch," Jens said. "Is this from that lady you're always daydreaming about?"

Nate's eyes flashed the direction Tory probably was, and all three of the guys laughed. Beckett clapped him on the shoulder a few times. "I guess you haven't kept your attraction to Tory on the down-low as much as you thought."

Nate shook his head, chuckling.

As Mrs. Davenport sang "Gloria, that color on you looks divine. Kiss him again, Barb— he's on cloud nine. All you kids get up and twirl and dance, and my, Edward, aren't you looking fine in those pants," Beckett waved them all in and put an arm around Nate, Jens, and Mark, prompting them all to do the same, like they were a football team in a huddle.

"What are we here for?" Beckett asked.

Nate said, "To entertain," at the same time Jens said, "To have fun."

Beckett grinned. "So let's ham it up out there. The winner gets dinner on me."

"And now," Mayor Stone said through the microphone, "let's hear it for the *Belt-it-out Builders!*"

As the first few notes of YMCA sounded over the speakers, all four of them jammed out while making their way up the stairs and onto the stage, to immediate cheers from the crowd. They had brainstormed a lot of different songs but had settled on YMCA because they figured it would be an easy song to get crowd participation.

That, and Jens said he played it on *Just Dance* with his daughter so many times that he could do it in his sleep, so they could just use that choreography. And maybe a few people in the crowd would know it, too.

They had all agreed that it would go best if they just went big on stage. If people were entertained enough, they weren't going to care if they sang off-tune or got some words wrong. So Nate went big. Much bigger than they had when they were practicing on the job site. He exaggerated all of the actions and threw in some extra little motions here and there, and the other three guys did the same.

The crowd was getting into it, too. Most of the people who had been sitting on blankets or lawn chairs were now standing, dancing along, and every time they did the chorus, everyone made the Y, M, C, and A letters with them.

Nate had forgotten how alive he felt when he was performing in front of a crowd, especially one as responsive as this. It made him smile even more broadly when he found Tory in the crowd, her kids all around her, all five of them dancing along and singing the chorus.

When it came time for Nate's dance solo while the others backed him up, all of them singing, Nate stepped forward and danced a solo aimed right at Tory. He had planned a few of his moves when they had been practicing earlier, but most of it he made up on the spot, just doing what came to him as he serenaded her with a song that was very much not a serenade. Not that he was putting on a show meant only for her or anything, but it was still a bold, risky move to do it in front of everyone when all eyes were on him. Had he thought about it ahead of time, he probably would've chickened out.

But when so much of his mind had been occupied by this one person, it just felt right. He was falling for her, and he didn't care if everyone knew.

Toward the end of his dance solo, he pointed at Tory with both hands. Without missing a beat, she responded by finishing the solo herself, the eyes of everyone there on her as they bounced along to the song. Her sense of rhythm and the ease at which she broke out the moves, never seeming unsure of what she was going to do next, told him that spontaneous dancing along to a song was something she did frequently. She pointed it back up to him at the end, and he rejoined the other three for the next part.

Back when he was married to Eva— if he had

somehow talked her into staying to watch— pulling a stunt like turning the dancing to her would've made her cross her arms, give a death glare that promised days of the silent treatment, and then storm off.

For the last chorus, the four of them put a hand cupped behind their ear, and the entire crowd sang along with them, all making the YMCA letters with their arms as they did. As he watched Tory and her kids singing and doing the actions, too, he realized that maybe his curse was done and over with. Maybe he no longer attracted— or was attracted to— the wrong person.

Maybe he was finally at a point where he could be with someone amazing.

thirteen

TORY

Tory watched Nate up on stage feeling like her heart was going to burst with happiness. Playfulness was one of the three most attractive qualities in a man, and she had never known that Nate had it at this high of a level. It made her want to spend more and more time with him, just to be able to get more chances to see it.

Nate and his crew were just so unforgettable up there, rocking out in their t-shirts and jeans and work boots and tool belts and hard hats. And the fact that he wore the flower crown that Aspen had made him while he was on stage in front of everyone made Aspen beam with pride and made Tory's heart melt.

While the Belt-it-out Builders had sung and danced, his eyes had often found hers, like a tie connecting them in the middle of this crowd.

And then when he'd been jamming out to his solo and turned it over to her, she had felt connected to him in a way that she hadn't felt connected to a man in a long time. At that moment, if he had motioned for her to come on stage to join him and at the end of their dance kissed her in front of everyone, she probably wouldn't have minded one bit.

———

After the sun set and the high school band, Flight of the Mountain Ducks, had finished the last note of their last song, Tory folded the blanket while her kids grabbed their baskets of goodies they'd gotten from the different activities.

"Did you walk here?" Nate asked.

Tory nodded.

"Can I walk you home?"

Tory was hoping that he would ask. She hadn't seen him nearly enough this evening for him to be going in the other direction to get into his truck and leave.

As they walked through the gate at the far side of the park, Tory carrying the blanket and Nate carrying the basket that held the picnic dinner they'd eaten before he arrived, her kids all got a little ahead of them. "So," Tory said, "between that dance and coming over to sit with us after it, it seems you have announced to the town your intention to start dating me."

Nate laughed uncomfortably, rubbing the back of his neck with his free hand. "I should've asked you if that was okay first. I got a little caught up in the moment and didn't consider that it might make things awkward for you. Please accept my apology."

Tory tried to hide a smile. The truth was she had enjoyed every second of it and had been rather flattered that he was willing to let everyone know that he had feelings for her. She understood what kind of bravery that took, and loved that he showed that kind of courage. But she was touched that he was considering it from her point of view. "Well, it depends, Nate Elsmore." He tensed. "Do you plan to date me?"

"Well, Tory Beckstead, that depends on whether or not you'll let me."

She smiled. "I'd like that." Then her eyes fell on her kids on the street in front of them. "I am worried about my kids, though. I haven't dated anyone since Trace and I'm concerned that they might..." She didn't quite know how to finish that sentence without being overly presumptuous.

Nate seemed to understand without her spelling it out. "They're with their dad on Fridays, right? What about Friday night?"

Covey ran back to Tory and said, "Can I have the house keys?"

Tory fished them out of her pocket and handed them to Covey, then he raced back to where his siblings were walking and skipping and bumping into each other and playing with some little toys they had won as they neared their house.

"Under one condition," Tory said to Nate as she stepped on to her lawn and her kids unlocked their front door and went inside. "You don't go back on that arm shake and you tell me your own embarrassing ex story."

Nate chuckled, shaking his head. "Friday night it is."

When they reached the front porch, Nate paused, studying Tory. "Thank you for asking me to come tonight. I needed that far more than I realized."

Tory looked into his eyes and felt like, for the first time, she was seeing two sides of him that molded seamlessly into a beautiful, intriguing man. Two sides that had always been there, but she'd never noticed. She wondered how many more sides of him she would get to know, and suddenly wanted to know them all.

Especially if they all came with these same beautiful brown eyes that were powerful yet soft, fiercely determined yet kind. Generous and giving and sincere. She wanted to reach out and touch those smile lines beside his eyes. And to run her fingertips down the scruff that he rarely wore but must've grown out for his performance. To touch those lips.

And suddenly she wished she didn't have a huge blanket folded in her arms, making a barrier between her and him.

Nate reached out and ran a single finger along her jawline, and she closed her eyes for a moment to soak in his touch. When she opened her eyes, she could tell by the way he was gazing at her face that he was just as hungry to reach out to her as she was to him. She shifted the blanket to her hip like it was a small child, and he shifted the basket he held to the other hand.

Keeping her eyes on his, she moved one step closer to him and breathed in his faint scent of amber, sawdust, and leather— so warm and rich, it drew her in closer. He reached out and skimmed his fingers down her upper arm, the touch leaving a line of thrill in its wake, then his eyes flicked to her lips, which made her eyes flick to his. Her heart sped up in anticipation, beating a quick staccato in her chest. He leaned in toward her and her lips parted ever so slightly.

Then the front door flew open, light spilling onto the porch, and Aspen said, "Mom, do you have my—"

Tory and Nate each took a step back quickly, and Nate tried to untangle the picnic basket from the edge of the blanket Tory held.

"Oh. I, um, sorry." Aspen giggled. "Never mind. I'm

good. You guys just...Bye!" Then she quickly shut the door.

Tory groaned. "That was..."

"Unexpected?" Nate offered.

"Sadly, it falls into the category of something I one hundred percent should have expected."

Nate reached out and squeezed her hand, then chuckled as the blinds in the window next to the door opened and three faces pressed against it. "I'll start sheetrocking tomorrow night." He handed her the picnic basket, giving her a smile that made her heart soar, and then started walking across her lawn back to the street. He turned just as he reached the road and added, "And I'll be thinking about Friday."

Tory watched him walk away until he was hidden by her neighbor's tree, then she went into her house, shut the door, and dropped the picnic basket and blanket.

Elodie tugged on her hand. "Were you and Nate kissing? I didn't see kissing, but Aspen said you were. Does this mean we're going to get an at-our-house dad? I really want a dad here, and I really like Nate. Do you think he'd be a good daddy? I think he'd be a good daddy. I think the chickens like him, too. And Cleopatrick. I mean, obviously. He stayed in his arms for like forever and he never does that."

"We're getting a new daddy?" Jackson asked.

"No," Tory said, hoping she hadn't made a mistake by choosing to date again. "Nate and I are going to go on a date and for now, that's it. Nothing more. You two are jumping way too far ahead of the game."

"We're playing a jumping game?" Jackson asked.

She chuckled and smiled big at her youngest. "We're done with games for tonight. Why don't you run upstairs and brush your teeth and get your pajamas on? Both of you."

As they raced each other up the stairs and to the bathroom, Tory leaned her back against the wall, letting out a giddy, contented sigh.

———

Tory woke up with a jolt Friday morning, knowing she was late before her brain consciously registered the fact that the sky was already lightening. She grabbed her phone off the night stand; the numbers 5:45 lit up and she panicked.

Racing into the girls' room, she shook both Aspen and Elodie. "Girls, hop up. My alarm didn't go off and we overslept." She turned their light on as she left the room, then ran into the boys' room and woke them up, too. "Hurry, up, up! The shop opens in," she glanced at the clock on the wall, "aaa! Thirteen minutes!"

Her kids had been raised on going to bed early and waking up early, so to have every single one of them accidentally sleep in this long rarely happened. She hurried back into her room, throwing on clothes, brushing her teeth, and trying in less than two minutes to make her hair and face not look like she had rolled out of bed moments ago, all while shouting instructions to her kids to do the same quickly and to grab their things.

"Everyone dressed?" she called out from her room. Everyone but Elodie had finished.

"Shoes on?"

"I can't find my shoes!" Jackson yelled back.

"Who's dressed, and has their shoes on and teeth brushed?" Tory asked as she slipped on her shoes and grabbed her bag.

"I am," Covey said. "I'll help him."

"Don't worry about hair," she called out. "We can do that at the shop. Just get your teeth brushed." She came out of her room, her bag in hand, shoving in makeup she likely wouldn't get a chance to put on, went into the kids' bathroom and added their brush and comb and a spray bottle of water to her bag, then came out and took an inventory of her kids. "Raise your hand if you've brushed your teeth."

Everyone raised their hand except Jackson, who was sitting on the floor, Covey tying his shoes.

"As soon as you're done, Jackson, brush. Everyone else, grab your backpacks and head out to the van."

As they raced to Love a Latte, Tory tried to calm her breathing. But it was already 6:01 when they pulled into the back parking lot, and she hadn't even started brewing the coffee yet. She got the kids inside, gave instructions to Covey and Aspen to get out the milk, cereal, paper bowls, and plastic spoons that they kept at the shop for days like today, and to make sure everyone ate, and then to get everyone's hair combed.

As they bustled around in their back room, Tory ran out front and started the coffee, then started loading up the cart. A glance outside in the predawn light told her that Broden Smith and Officer Banks had already shown up for their morning wake-up call. She piled supplies onto the cart as quickly as she could grab them, grabbed the money belt and the credit card reader, and pushed the cart to the table out front.

"Good morning, boys!" she called out, trying to force her normal happy-to-greet-customers self out into the open, and shove the crazy, unorganized mom stress onto the back burner. "What can I get for you this fine morning?"

They both ordered coffees, so she rang them up, taking time to slow her frayed nerves and leisurely chat as she did so the coffee would have time to finish. Then she went inside, switched the half-filled pot with a new one and filled their cups, then started a second machine before taking their coffees back out in front of the store.

Tory wished she could go back inside to finish getting all the coffees started, but a couple of Main Street business owners were already on the sidewalks, headed her way. So she just wrapped her arms around herself and wished that she had remembered to grab the jacket that was still home on the hook that she always wore in these early mornings before the sun rose.

The morning brought a near-constant stream of customers, and an almost constant stream of her kids coming outside to ask questions or tell her things or ask for her help. She couldn't wait to spend her mornings back inside the shop, because then it made it so much easier to check on them often and be there for everything they needed.

"Mom," Covey said, pushing the front door open. "Someone's knocking on the back door. Should I open it?"

There was a small break in customers, so Tory rushed inside and through the Employees Only door and down the hallway to the back door. She opened it to a man dressed in white zip-up coveralls, tools, and a bucket of sheetrock mud in his hands.

She hadn't remembered until that moment that Nate had told her that the electricians at one of his sites had run into a problem that delayed the sheetrockers, which freed up a sub-contractor to come do the sheetrock mud and tape in her shop today.

"Oh! Hello, come on in." She led him to the lobby. "I'll be out front— let me know if you need anything from me." Then she rushed back up front to help the couple of people who were now waiting at her little outdoor stand.

By the time eight rolled around, she felt like she'd run a marathon. She brought the cart inside, locked the front door and put up the "Will reopen at 8:20" sign, and turned to see Elodie and Jackson drawing pictures on the plywood floor with some of the sheetrock mud that had dropped. Both of them had big sections of white powder on their clothes from rubbing up against the sheetrock edges and from sitting on the floor covered with the stuff. She hurried to get them cleaned up, then had everyone grab their backpacks and quickly get into the van.

She had barely gotten back to the shop from dropping them off at school and gotten her cart back outside, helping the customers who had lined up while she was gone, before she got a call from Jackson's teacher. Her friend Alete was at the front of the line, so she said, "Sorry!" and answered the call.

"Hi, Tory. As you know, it's Jackson's turn to bring the snacks today. He says he knows you bought them, but that maybe they were still at your house, so I thought I'd check in with you."

Tory put her palm on her forehead. "Oh my goodness. Yes, I bought them, but they're sitting on my kitchen table so we wouldn't forget them. I, um..." Her mind raced, trying to figure out how she was going to get them to the school. "I'll get them to you as soon as I can." She hung up the phone and took a deep breath.

"What'd ya forget?" Alete asked.

"Snacks for Jackson's class." Tory turned to the table behind her and prepared Alete's French vanilla latte.

When she turned to hand it to Alete, the woman said, "I can get them and take them to the school."

"You will?" Tory came around the table that was functioning as her front counter and wrapped her arms around Alete, relief and stress pouring out of her. Then she grabbed her keys from the cart and pressed them into Alete's hands. "This is my house key. It's the grocery bag on the table, and you can just drop them off at the front office. Thank you, thank you, Alete. I owe you a massive favor, and I expect you to call it in some time."

As Alete left with her keys, she blew out a long, slow breath before turning to the next customer. Her life was too crazy, too chaotic, too much of a mess. What made her think that it was okay to go on a date tonight? She shouldn't be introducing something more into her life, like starting to date someone, when she couldn't even manage all the things that were in her life already.

Dating Nate is crazy and irresponsible, she told herself.

And then Nate stepped into her line, and her stomach filled with butterflies and her heart rose like a helium balloon and a smile spread across her face.

Maybe it wasn't *so* irresponsible. Maybe a little crazy was good. Maybe, just maybe, she could find a way to make it all work.

NATE

ate had been a one-cream, one-sugar kind of coffee drinker for practically his entire adult life. But lately, he found himself craving a visit to the sold-from-the-sidewalk version of Love a Latte to see what Tory thought was the drink he most needed every morning. And every morning the drink was perfect.

At least he told himself it was the drink and not just the woman serving it. He knew a lot of people who thought the day just went better if it started with a cup of coffee, but he found his day went better when he started it with Tory.

That morning when he had stopped at Love a Latte, he had been trying to decide between two different date ideas and asked if she liked adventure, which of course she said yes to. Then he asked if she wanted to do a ropes course, and she seemed excited by the idea. He had been hoping that would be the case.

"Nate. *Nate.*"

His head jerked up to see his brother trying to get his attention from the other end of the four-foot by eight-foot sheet of plywood they were nailing to the side of a home.

"You can let go now."

He looked at his brother, confused.

"I already nailed that side you're 'holding' up."

Embarrassed, Nate let go. Tory had occupied his mind all day long. So much so that he could hardly focus on the job most of the day. He had to keep taking breaks several times a day to refer back to his master schedule of all the homes in progress and had to re-figure out which ones needed extra help when usually that kind of information he always just had in his head.

And then there were embarrassing moments like this when someone witnessed exactly how distracted he was by thoughts of her. It had been a long week, and tonight wasn't coming nearly quickly enough.

———

Nate opened the car door for Tory after he parked at the Mountain Springs Outdoor Adventure Park. She stepped out of the car wearing ordinary jeans, a t-shirt, and gym shoes that somehow had taken on an extraordinary quality when she had put them on.

She looked around at the area, taking it in. "Have you ever been here before?"

He shut her door and put his hand on the small of her back, motioning her toward the main building. "Yeah, we came here for a family activity last summer. Me, my sister Jeigh, my brother Beckett, and his wife Kimberly all did the ropes course while my parents took pictures. It was a lot of fun— I think you'll like it."

After he paid for the course, they hopped on a double-seater golf cart driven by a teenaged boy and went up the winding mountain path to the course. When they stepped off the cart, the sun was setting and Tory looked up at the impressive structure with the backdrop of a beautiful sunset.

The framework was all made of wood— huge round wooden pillars rising into the sky were connected by each of the ropes challenges. There were two courses— one was just a small flight of stairs above the path they stood on, and one was fifteen feet above that. Since it was on the side of a mountain, though, the lower course was about ten feet above the ground on the side close to the path and a good twenty-five or thirty feet above the ground along the backside.

"This is it?" Tory asked.

Nate grinned, remembering how much fun he'd had on it before.

"When you said 'ropes course' I had pictured something on the ground. Like an obstacle course they show in army movies."

"Oh, no. This is much better than that." But then he looked at Tory's face and saw trepidation. "Or maybe it's not. Do you not want to do this? We don't have to."

Tory scoffed. "Are you kidding? Balance is my friend. It never lets me down." She winked at him, then grabbed his hand and pulled him to the worker standing by the harnesses.

Nate grabbed a harness for Tory and held it out while she stepped into it. Then he helped her get the strap over her shoulders and buckled in all the right places. He snugged up a few of the straps and then tugged on the ring at the front where the tether would connect. "Feel good?"

Tory nodded and gave him two thumbs up, so he got his harness on while she grabbed each of them a helmet just as giant floodlights from high above were turned on and shone down on the course.

After getting some instruction from the woman at the base of the stairs, Tory strutted up the stairs, looking confident as could be. Something was off, though, but he couldn't put his finger on what. "You first," she said, both arms motioning toward the course, a big grin on her face. "Show me how it's done."

The woman manning the course hooked the tether up to Nate's harness, checked it, told him he could head out, and then she did the same for Tory. The first obstacle was nice and easy. It had wide, flat boards to step on, each step connected by ropes on both sides, with cables running at waist height on both sides to use as handrails when going across. He had only taken the first few steps before Tory called out, "Come on, I've seen bad news travel faster than that!"

He chuckled. "Well, you know me, I'm *high* maintenance."

"I saw that wobble. Are you a little woozy from all the fresh air up here?"

"Yeah. It's giving me a natural high." Nate finished walking across it, then stepped onto the platform around the pillar and turned to watch Tory.

She was a little slower than he was, taking each step carefully, testing it first to make sure it was safe, never fully releasing her grip on the cables as she moved forward. "My mama always said that slow and steady wins the race."

"And I see you're taking that to heart."

Tory chuckled, but the sound came out a little more nervous than he was expecting. The step up to the platform was a big one, so as she neared, he wrapped one arm around the pillar and reached out with the other. She hesitated for a moment, then reached out and grabbed his arm, and he pulled her to him, and she grabbed hold of his waist with one arm and the pillar with the other.

"Tory, are you afraid of heights?"

"No, *your mom* is—" Tory started off the joke in typical "your mom" joke fashion, but ended with "a very nice person. I really like her."

Nate smiled. "You ready for the next one?"

"Only if you go faster than you did on the last one. That was about as exciting as watching grass grow." She winked and gave him a little squeeze before releasing him and wrapping her other arm around the post.

This next challenge turned away from the road, so the ground was dropping off rapidly below them. It was a twenty-foot-long horizontal log lying stretched out between the pillar they were at and the next, with no cable to hold on to.

Of course, he could hold on to the safety tether that connected to the cables above, but since it moved as much as he did, he'd learned the first time he came that it was only helpful to give him something to hold onto, not to aid in getting across the challenge. So this time he just put his arms straight out to the sides for balance, walking slowly across.

"I've seen better form from kids walking down the curb at my kids' school," Tory called out.

"Just give me a moment," Nate said. "I'm just looking for something I lost."

"What did you lose?"

"My balance."

"Ha ha," Tory said. "You've reached new *heights* with that one."

Nate laughed and tried not to lose his balance for real from the motion. He finally made it to the other side, stepped up on to the platform, and turned to see Tory. Her eyes weren't on him— they were on the log she needed to step down on. She was holding so tightly to the tether, he was sure that the individual twisting coils in it were imprinted in her palms.

"That first step down is the worst one. Once you get onto the log, it isn't bad at all."

"But there's nothing to hold on to!"

"Just keep holding the tether if it helps. And remember that you can't fall no matter what you do."

She nodded but didn't take her eyes off where her feet needed to go on the log. With tensed muscles, she slowly lowered one foot onto the log.

"You can do it, Tory."

She stepped the other foot down, and her tether started shaking—probably because her arms were trembling. Without lifting her foot, she slid it forward inch by inch, and Nate held his breath for her. Very slowly, she made it nearly three feet away from the platform. Then she screamed. "Nate, I can't do this, I can't do this! All that trash talk was a smokescreen to hide the fact that I'm terrified of heights!"

Nate stepped down onto the log and walked across it to her as quickly as he could, his arms forward the entire way as if he could catch her if she fell. She was trembling violently, terror in her eyes, barely breathing. When he reached her, he put a hand on each hip and held her tight so she would know she was safe and wouldn't fall. It took her a moment to convince herself to pry a hand loose from her tether, but she did and put the trembling hand on his shoulder, her fingers gripping him tightly.

"Tory, I'm so sorry. I had no idea you were afraid of heights. We can go back."

Tory glanced over her shoulder— gripping him tighter with the motion—to where a family was crossing the challenge between them and the beginning of the course. She squeezed her eyes shut.

"It doesn't matter," Nate said. "We can get you back on that platform, wait for them to pass, and then go back."

She opened her eyes again, and glanced at the rest of the course, then looked back at Nate. "No, let's keep going."

"Tory—"

"No," she said more forcefully. "We're not going back.

I always joke that I'm not afraid of heights; I'm only afraid of falling. This," she tugged on her tether, "will keep me from falling, and being afraid of heights without falling is stupid." She took in a slow, shaky breath. "It's not real. I won't fall. I can do this."

He studied her eyes and saw a depth of determination he wasn't sure he'd ever seen in another human before. So he gave her a nod. "Okay, we'll do this together. I'm not going to let go of you. See? I've got you held tight. Just keep holding onto my shoulder and keep your eyes on mine. Don't look down, because down is irrelevant. All that matters is across, okay?"

She nodded, the motion slight. But her eyes didn't leave his.

"Right foot first." He moved his left foot backward as she slid her right foot forward. "Good. Okay, now left foot."

They moved across the log slowly, Nate going backward for the first time, making sure his footing was good, even though he wasn't able to see where he was going. He didn't want to make a move that would cause him to lose his balance when Tory was relying on his stability so much.

When his right ankle slid onto the platform on the other side, he said, "I'm going to let go of your right hip and hold on to your right hand so I can step onto the platform and then help you up. Is that okay?" She nodded, so he made the switch, then turned his body so he could step up, then pulled her up onto the platform to him.

This time, she held on to him with both arms around his waist. Her first few breaths were deep and trembling. But then she whispered, "Thank you."

"Do you want to keep going, or head back? Either is fine with me."

"Keep going." She nodded her head at the next challenge. Two strong cables at shoulder height gave something to hold onto, and bendy ropes came down in U-shapes from it, giving something to step on as they made their way across. "But as we go across, you're going to have to tell me your divorce story to distract me from the fact that we're—" she glanced down at the weeds and shrubs growing out of the mountainside below, "like fifty feet above the ground here."

"Fair enough." He stepped onto the next challenge backward so he could face Tory. He didn't have a phobia of heights, but that didn't mean he was fearless this high off the ground, with only a one-inch thick rope separating him and the depths below.

While taking a step back, trying to find the rope with his foot, he thought through how and what to tell Tory. Talking about his divorce was tough enough, and he'd honestly never dreamed he'd have to do it while walking backward on a ropes course high in the air.

He waited until Tory put a shaky foot down onto the

first rope and lowered herself until it held her weight completely, then slowly moved her other foot onto the rope in front of it. Her legs shook, making the ropes swing back and forth, and panic hit her.

"Eyes on mine, Tory."

Her eyes flew to his. "Talk, please."

"Okay. Um, I started Elsmore Construction straight out of college and started dating Eva about a year later. We dated for about two years before getting married. I would've loved to be married sooner, but I needed to make sure my construction company was doing well enough so I could support us."

He took another step back, his foot fishing for the next rope. As he leaned his weight back onto that leg, Tory took another shaky step onto the next rope, her hands still gripping the cables tightly.

"It wasn't until much later that I looked back and realized that I would've been fine living with the income I was making back then. It had been Eva who had planted the thought, and had somehow made me believe it was mine."

Another step back for him and another step forward for Tory, like they were connected. He could see that his talking calmed her, so he tried to not pause to think about what to say next.

"We bought a house that was a little too big, but Eva loved it and I wanted to make her happy." He stepped back. "She didn't end up being happy, though. There were so many areas in which I was lacking, and I was constantly trying to be better— a better husband, a better wage-earner, a better person— but it always just seemed out of reach.

"I thought maybe if I could figure out how to do everything right, and then she would be willing to start a family. I had been working for it for so long, and I just wanted to be a dad and experience familial bliss. But I always fell short."

His foot slipped off a rope, and his grip on the cables caught him. As he reached back with one foot to catch the rope again, his front foot swung forward bumping into Tory's. She stiffened, every muscle strained, wrapping her arms around the cables, locking her knees, holding her breath.

Her legs were trembling, though, then violently shaking, and soon the rope her forward leg was on swung forward and the other backward, making neither beneath her enough to hold her weight. She fought and strained, grasping onto the cables at her shoulders, desperately trying to wrap her arms around them, and managed to pull both legs back to where they should be, leaving her breathing in big, heaving gasps.

Finally, as he twisted to see behind him, he found the rope and got his foot placed on it correctly and his balance was restored. "It's okay, we're good. Are you good?"

Tory gave a tense nod, took a few deep breaths, and then said in a barely audible, strained voice, "Tell me what happened next."

Nate calmed his breathing and took another step back, trying to refocus, then said, "Well, that caused a lot of friction in our marriage, and eventually she got impatient waiting for me to be the man she knew I could be and decided that she was going to go stay with her sister in Oakland for a couple of months to give me the motivation to be better."

He drank in the look on Tory's face as his foot found the rope behind him. It was one of disbelief and confusion, not one of judgment. "Eva had taken my heart with her, but after the initial pain of her leaving, I realized how much happier I was when she wasn't around, and how much more I believed in myself. It also helped me to realize, or at least start to realize, how many of my thoughts weren't mine at all. They had been planted by Eva."

He reached the next platform, and maneuvered around on the last rope, to get where he was facing the platform, and then stepped up on it, holding out a hand toward Tory as she took the last few steps, then reached for his hand and joined him on the platform.

She let out a deep, smiling breath. "We made it past another one."

"We did," he said. "And you did great. You only looked down once."

"Twice. But who's counting."

As they went through the next several challenges—tough ones that took a little more focus, Tory seemed to slowly gain confidence. She kept asking questions about him and Eva to help distract her, so he told her about how once he started to realize how much he was being manipulated, his conversations with her had taken on a whole new light and he finally understood that she never wanted children. She simply knew it was the most effective carrot to dangle in front of him.

Nate told Tory that as Eva had noticed that he was beginning to wake up to her methods, she suddenly wanted to get back together. He said no, but he came home from a site one day and found that she had moved back in. The difference in the feeling in their house had been drastic, and he knew right then that he couldn't spend the rest of his life under her control and feeling like he would never be good enough.

As he pulled Tory onto the platform next to him, she said, "Oh, Nate. I am so sorry you had to go through that." She searched his eyes, and he felt like she was seeing right into him. "Relationships with manipulators can be hard to escape from. And even harder to recover from. You must've worked hard to get where you're at."

He really had. It made heat spread through his chest that she noticed.

"Nate!" she said, tugging on his shirt. "We made it to the last challenge!" She turned around on the platform, gazing back over all the challenges they had done, a look of wonder on her face.

"Come on," he said, grinning. "Let's get to it."

The last challenge had a single one-inch metal cable running between the platforms that they had to walk across. Instead of any kind of cable or rope to hang on to, about every four or five feet, a pole hung from a cable above that was low enough to grab hold of. The poles swung back and forth in the slight breeze, showing that they weren't going to be something stable to hold on to, and Tory's eyes were glued to them.

"We'll have to face the side on this one," she said.

He nodded and stepped down onto the cable, stretching to reach the first pole. After inching along a bit further, he switched the pole to his right hand and then reached for the next one with his left hand. A moment later, the cable pulled up slightly as Tory stepped down on it. He knew from last time that ones like this were much easier if only one person was on it at a time, but he was glad he was doing it by Tory's side.

She had decided to face the other direction, so they could see each other a little easier as they went. Whenever Nate wasn't reaching for a pole, he looked at Tory, checking to make sure she was okay. She was concentrating hard on sliding her feet across the cable, making sure her movements didn't make it bounce, keeping her knees slightly bent, and not losing balance as she reached out for each new pole. The terror from earlier was gone, and all that was left now was sheer determination.

"Are you ready for me to step off?" Nate asked when he reached the end. He knew that the cable would shift for her as soon as he did.

She nodded and braced herself, holding on to two of the poles. The dip in the cable bounced her a bit, but she kept her balance and recovered. Soon, she made her way to the end and stepped up onto the big ending platform without his help. She took two steps away from the edge, then jumped up and down and wrapped her arms around him in a hug. He sensed how huge this was for her, and felt every bit of excitement right along with her.

Tory marched right up to the end of the wooden platform and leaned out over the drop-off below, her arms straight at her sides, her hands in fists. "Take that!" she yelled to the mountainside far below.

Then she turned back to Nate. "Nate, I did it. I did it! I really did it! All of them!" She walked to the edge, looking down the mountain, and then walked back. "My fear of heights has kept me from trying so many things ever since I was a little kid. But you— you helped me conquer it." She stepped up close to him, just inches separating them. "I never could have done any of this without you."

With one hand still on his tether, he reached out and pressed the release button on her helmet strap. She took her helmet off and dropped it at their feet, and he did the same with his. "You," he said, tucking a lock of hair back into her ponytail, "are incredible. I'm pretty sure there is nothing that could stand in your way that you couldn't conquer." He stared into her eyes, marveling at the fire that burned within them. At features that were somehow both strong and soft, fierce and resolute, caring and powerful.

He ran a hand down the arm he had held onto so many times throughout the course, then dropped his grip on his tether and moved both hands to her hips, where they had held her and kept her steady. She reached between them and unhooked each of their carabineers that held their tethers, and pushed the tethers down their pathway toward the woman who had connected them to their harnesses at the beginning, and then she moved in even closer to him.

"And you," she said, wrapping her hands behind his neck and running her fingertips through his hair, causing chills to race down his back, "are patient and caring and brilliant at talking a girl through the worst panic attack she's had in her life. Never could I have guessed that the moment when I would feel most safe in my life was when I was standing on a cable thirty feet up in the air."

She lightly rubbed little circles behind his ears with her thumbs, which made him go crazy with anticipation. He had been thinking about kissing her nonstop since their almost-kiss five days earlier, and he couldn't keep his eyes off her lips.

Tory rose on her toes and pulled him toward her. His lips met hers, and the fire and determination that had been burning within her burst through the kiss, and he suddenly felt more alive than he had ever felt. Energy coursed through him, making his fingers tingle and the hairs on his arms stand out straight.

He moved one hand to the small of her back, and slid the other up toward her neck, pulling her close, and she slid her hand further into his hair, pulling him just as closely to her.

They deepened the kiss, and he held her tight, wishing they could stay like that forever. Eventually, his kiss turned into a smile, and he felt hers do the same.

"Wow," she whispered against his lips. "We should definitely do that again soon."

Movement from the corner of his eye caught Nate's attention, and he turned his head to see that one of the kids from the family behind them on the course— probably a ten or eleven-year-old— was looking up at them curiously.

Nate cleared his throat, then he and Tory separated a bit. Nate turned to the parents, mouthed *Sorry*, then bent down and picked up his and Tory's helmets. Then he led the strongest woman he'd ever met down the stairs and to the area where they could return their harnesses.

TORY

Saturday morning, Tory woke up giddy about Nate. All morning long, she whistled as she bathed Nacho, pet Cleopatrick, went grocery shopping, and did load after load of laundry. She couldn't stop thinking about how it had felt to have his hands on her hips, his soft voice at her ear, her hands on his strong shoulders. But more than that, she was amazed at how safe she'd felt with him.

She hadn't just felt safe with him physically, although there were many times throughout the ropes course when she was convinced that his guiding hands were the only thing keeping her from falling. But for the first time, she'd felt like her hopes, dreams, fears, ambitions, and worries would all be just as safe with him.

Since Trace was all about fun and games, he had always laughed at her fear of heights, making jokes about it and teasing her incessantly for it, making her feel like it was such a deficiency in her character. She had always fought back with words, in the same joking tone he had used.

It was probably why she had resorted to trash talk when she was faced with the terror of the ropes course with Nate. The way Trace had dealt with her fear usually caused her to hide it in shame whenever possible— he definitely hadn't given her space to grow and overcome it.

But Nate had. Instead of teasing, he showed care and concern, and even a willingness to back out and do something else instead. And when he saw that instead, she wanted to fight and overcome, he picked up his sword and fought alongside her, watching her back.

When her kids finally got home just before noon, they all raced into the house, excited to tell her about their night spent at a family fun center in Mountain Springs. Once they had exhausted all talk of rides and arcade games and go-carts and laser tag and miniature golf and dug into the lunch she had prepared, Elodie said around a bite of her sandwich, "How was your fun night with Nate?"

Tory grinned widely. She didn't want to get into the more date-ish parts of the date with them, but she did want to talk about the activity. "He took me to a ropes course on the side of a mountain, and there was one part where I was standing on a cable that was only this big around, and I was thirty feet off the ground!" Her kids' eyes were wide—they all knew how afraid of heights she was.

"Did you scream and run away?" Jackson asked.

She shook her head and told them the story. She didn't hold back on the details of how terrified she had been, how she had gotten through it, or how victorious she had felt at the end of the course. It was important to her that her kids saw examples of people facing hard things and overcoming them, and she hoped her story would inspire them. Based on how closely they'd all been listening as she had told the story, she knew it would at least stick with them.

"So," Aspen said as Tory finished her story, "at the end of the date did you kiss him?" Then she and Elodie and Jackson all started making kissy noises. Covey, though, scowled, pushed his chair back, and stormed off, stomping up the stairs to his room.

"That," Tory said with a wink, "is none of your business. I need to go talk with Covey for a bit— will you three decide which Saturday chores game we should play today? Look at the list, and then figure out which one together. Remember that we have soccer games in two hours, so chose one that won't take too long."

As Tory walked up the stairs, she heard muttering coming from Covey's room, and it didn't sound happy. Most of it she couldn't hear, but as she rounded the hall to his doorway, she heard, "He's ruining everything."

"Can I come in?" she asked.

Covey nodded, but he didn't take his eyes off his lap. She shut the door behind her, and then sat on Jackson's bed, facing Covey's.

"You sound pretty upset."

He nodded, but still didn't meet her eyes. "'Cause, you're cheating on Dad."

Tory's eyebrows raised in shock. "Honey, I *can't* cheat on Dad because he and I aren't together." This was a side of dating that she hadn't seen coming. She probably should have, though. It couldn't be easy for them to accept that their mom was seeing someone when that someone could potentially one day move into their lives.

Covey raised his head. "But you could be."

"No, sweetie, we can't. And believe me, we tried for a very long time to make it work."

"Things weren't so bad when Dad lived here. Why can't we just go back to the way things were? I liked it when I could see both of my parents at the same time. When we would sit down for dinner with all of us. When we would play games together. And when we would get to Love a Latte after school, you and Dad would both be there."

Tory nodded, not knowing how to say the "Yes, but..." part.

"You can make it that way again," Covey said, his voice full of hopefulness.

She took a slow, deep breath. "It is nice to think about all the good times we had with Dad. I really liked all those times, too. But Covey, there were also a lot of issues we had that we both tried hard to fix, and we couldn't."

"Dad still wants to be married to you."

"He doesn't. In the end, honey, your dad decided that even though he loves you all and always wants to be with you, he didn't want to stay married to me." She reminded all of her kids frequently that the divorce wasn't because of them. Never had she brought up fault when it came to the divorce before, though, and she wasn't about to start now. But she did feel like maybe it was important to let Covey know that it was Trace who had decided to call it quits.

She groaned inwardly. How had they been divorced for a year and a half and she still hadn't figured out how to share this part with her kids? She knew it would come at some point. "And that's why he started dating Kennedy. Because he found someone who he won't have those same issues with. He has decided that he wants to be with her."

Covey shook his head. "Nope. They broke up."

The shock hit Tory hard. Tory hadn't seen the two of them together often, but Trace had still seemed smitten with her. What had happened? *When* had it happened? Had Kennedy just been so much quicker than Tory had been at figuring out that Trace was never going to be responsible? If she had known this news, she probably would've gone about this conversation a little differently.

"So nothing is stopping you and Dad from getting back together. He said he still loves you."

Tory breathed in slowly. She was going to have to talk to Trace about not saying things like that to the kids. It was cruel to make their kids think there was a chance to have their parents together in one big happy family when there so obviously wasn't. When he came to pick up the kids next Friday, she was going to have her kids wait inside while she had a little chat with him outside, and they would have to agree on some ground rules. It wasn't fair to make their son hurt like this.

"Honey," she said and moved to sit next to him on his bed. "I know this is hard. I get it—I really do. I need you to understand, though, that your dad and I are not getting back together. That decision has already been made, by both of us. Breaking up with someone hurts a lot, right here," she said, touching her heart, "and I think your dad is just hurting right now because he and Kennedy broke up. He's saying those things about me because it makes the breakup with her a little less painful, but it doesn't make them true.

"And if you're sad that they broke up, and you're missing Kennedy, it's okay if you're hurting right here, too."

"I'm not missing Kennedy— I am missing having my

parents be married to each other. That's what I really want."

Tory wrapped her arms around her son, stroking his hair with one hand. "I know, Covey. Divorce is so, so hard. I hope that one day it gets easier for you and for all of us."

And then she held him as he silently cried into her side.

sixteen

NATE

Nate stopped in to Love a Latte Tuesday morning before work. There were three people in line in front of him on the sidewalk, but he didn't mind. It gave him a chance to just watch how Tory interacted with people. She chatted and laughed and commiserated and asked about things happening in people's lives, and every one of them walked away with a bigger smile on their faces than they had when they'd arrived.

When it was his turn at the folding table under the awning, a smile lit up Tory's face that made all his worries lighten. He was glad that no one had gotten in line behind him yet, so he could have a few more minutes with her.

"Good morning," he said, wishing this table wasn't between them so he could reach out and pull her into a morning embrace. If he could, he would kiss her right here at the heart of Main Street, and he wouldn't care who witnessed it.

"Good morning," she said. His hands were on the table, and she reached out and put one of hers on top of his, and it made his pulse quicken. "Who's choosing your drink this morning?"

He grinned. "You."

"All right," she said, folding her arms and leaning back a bit, studying him. "What do you have going on today?"

"I do a check on all the properties we're working on every Tuesday. And then this afternoon, I've got to head to Mountain Springs for a final walk-through on our first finished house of the season."

"That's exciting! Congratulations!"

He glanced up at the awning. "What would you say to this being your last day serving coffee outside?"

She looked at him, her eyes wide in shock and disbelief. "What? How?"

He lifted a shoulder in a shrug, a smile playing at his lips. "I got all the new walls primed last night. Tonight after I'm done working, I can come in and paint. I could stop by early tomorrow morning and put on outlet covers.

"There's still a lot to do, of course. Trim, flooring, lighting, and practically everything on the outside of the building, so we're far from finished. But if you want, things will be done enough inside for code, so you can open. Unless, of course, you want to wait until you can do a grand re-opening."

"Oh, Nate!" She ran around to the outside of the table and wrapped him in a hug. He put his arms around her waist and breathed in deeply, relishing the feel of her in his arms, her breath at his neck. "I can't believe how much you've accomplished in such a short amount of time. You are incredible."

He smiled, trying not to burst any buttons on his flannel shirt. "So I take it you don't want to wait for a grand re-opening?"

Tory laughed as she headed behind the counter and started making him a drink. "Oh, I'm not saying I won't do one. But I'm not about to turn down the chance to run a coffee shop from the inside of a building instead of on a sidewalk." She finished making his drink, then turned and put it on the table between them.

He raised his eyebrows. "A cinnamon dolce latte? With an extra shot of espresso?"

"I looked in deeply and saw that's what you needed today. It's not my job to guess why." She shrugged and then winked. "But if I had to hazard a guess, I'd say it is because of how much you have planned today. Nate, I've painted plenty of rooms in my house, and it always takes so much longer than I thought it would. Are you sure there's time for that tonight?"

He nodded. "It's not too much more work than

priming is. And last night I was finished with the priming by nine. It won't be a problem."

"I wish I could come to help you. Tonight's just too packed."

"I wish you could come, too." A smile spread across his lips. "But with as much as I want to kiss you again like we did at the ropes course, I think having you there to help would actually take longer."

Tory laughed, and then leaned right across the table and kissed him, in plain view of anyone who happened to be looking their direction in the early morning hours. He smiled and then stole one more quick peck. "Have a wonderful day."

"You, too," she said and watched him walk to his truck.

seventeen

TORY

ory had just gotten her kids and their backpacks out of Love a Latte Tuesday afternoon and buckled into the van, ready to back out of her parking spot, when she got a text from Katie.

> Katie: Have you driven very far?
> Someone just brought a surprise in here
> for you.

She took the keys out of the ignition, and said, "Stay in your seats—I'll be right back," then she unlocked the back door of Love a Latte and went inside. When she got to the front of the store, she spotted a big bouquet of bright, colorful flowers, and her heart melted.

While she was admiring how beautiful and sweet and thoughtful each one was, Ruth came inside the lobby and said, "We told the guy that we were texting you to come back, so he's just out front with Katie, checking out how the front of the building was coming along while he waited."

Tory smiled and picked up the card that was nestled into the greenery, and opened it.

Dear Tory,
I've been thinking about you nonstop and hope you're willing to give us a second chance.
Love, Trace

They were from *Trace?* Tory scowled at the card and then tossed it to the counter. She was ready to march outside and tell him what she thought of his stunt when he walked right in through the front door. He put his sunglasses on the back of his neck, brushed his hair off to the side, and smiled widely. She stormed right up to him.

"Trace, bringing me flowers is not okay."

"Tory, not here. We have customers right outside the window."

We?

She was willing to have this discussion anywhere, so she took a step toward the front door, but he brushed past her and headed for the Employees Only door.

"Trace!" she called out behind him. "You're not an employee!"

He still went into the back, though, like he still co-owned the place. He didn't stop at her office like she thought he would— he went straight out the back door, stopping in the parking lot in full view of her van full of their kids.

"Tory, I miss you," he said, reaching out like he was going to tuck a lock of hair behind her ear, but she batted his hand away.

"You do not. Listen, I'm sorry to hear that you and Kennedy broke up. Truly, I am. But it is not okay to come running back to me just because you're feeling a little lonely."

"It's more than that, Tory." He took a step closer to her. "We were good together. We can be good together again. We were married for ten years, Tor. It's a shame to throw that all away."

Tory took a step back, knowing full well that Covey was seeing all this, crossing both his fingers that they would decide to be married again right this second, and if they didn't, he'd believe it was all her fault, and that made her angry.

"We had some good times," Tory said. "But we were *not* good together. We brought out the worst in each other, and I wouldn't want to inflict that on either of us ever again."

"Maybe in the past. But we've grown, and I think we could make it work this time. Let me come home with you and we can talk about it."

Tory shook her head. "Covey has piano lessons in fifteen minutes, and then I have to go straight from there to soccer practice with the other kids. Then I'm making dinner for a neighbor and all the kids have play dates, at my house. Then homework and baths and bed. But even if I wasn't busy, we wouldn't need to talk this out, Trace. You *should* be with someone. You *should* have a woman in your life."

Trace opened his mouth to say something, but she didn't give him a chance.

"But it's not me. Trace, I am the one person on this earth that you *know* you can't be happy with. Go and find anybody else."

Then she walked back to her van and paused with her hand on the door. "Oh, and stop telling the kids that you want to get back together with me, or that you still love me. It's not fair to them." Then she got into her van and backed out of her spot, hands trembling, ignoring him still standing in front of where she'd been parked, his hand outstretched toward her.

NATE

Early in the spring, before the days had gotten warmer and before the snow had melted, Nate had started lining up his construction jobs for the spring, summer, and fall. It was easy to see it was going to be a busy year from the start. He was quick to go to other construction companies throughout the state that he had relationships with to see if any had an abundance of crew that they would be willing to loan to his crew for a percentage.

Once he'd gotten a taker, he lined up jobs for Elsmore Construction until he got to the point of turning everyone else away, all assuming the new crew size.

Which, in hindsight, had been a terrible idea, and they were to the point in the season when they were feeling it. All of his crew had agreed to the extra hours because the overtime money was so great, but they were starting to tire, and there were still many months left. It was also the time in the season when things started to go wrong, sending his schedule into chaos. He had been around long enough to know to anticipate it, but he'd never had to adjust to such a tight job-to-crew ratio.

On his way to Mountain Springs to do the scheduled walk-through with the new owners to make a punch list of last-minute things that needed to be fixed, his mind tried to run through ways to deal with his shortage of workers but instead kept wandering to Tory. He kept forcing it back to the task at hand, but really, it was just so much more enjoyable to think of her, so sometimes his mind fought back.

He arrived at the home early, but the future homeowners were already on the front porch, the wife standing with her arms crossed and her foot tapping, and the husband sitting on a window sill, his hands on the sill, his body leaning forward. This was not good. He got out of his truck and walked up the recently poured sidewalks, forcing a pleasant expression on his face. "You both don't look thrilled. Are things inside all finished?"

"No," the woman huffed. "Things are so far from being finished, it's downright criminal. And we're supposed to sign the papers tomorrow and have movers set to move us in over the weekend."

Dread filled Nate's stomach. He prided himself on

Elsmore Construction finishing jobs on time and correctly. It sounded like one of the two things might not be happening, and that was against everything he stood for. And if things were massively wrong inside, he wasn't sure how he was going to find the man-hours to fix it.

He didn't know how things could be so bad, though— he hadn't checked in on the Mountain Springs homes as often as the Nestled Hollow ones, but he'd been in this house just last Thursday, and everything had been on track. "Well, let's go inside and see what we're dealing with, then."

As they walked through the home, the couple pointed out all the little things that were wrong. There were a good amount of little things, but he kept preparing himself for the huge issues— the 'downright criminal' things— and they never appeared.

The way the woman talked about each of the items, though, reminded him so much of the way that Eva used to talk to him, and the feel of the home with this couple in it reminded him how his and Eva's entire world had felt. Cold, oppressive, and destructive.

Each time one of them pointed out another flaw—a place where paint needed to be fixed, a nail hole showing, a missed spot of caulking, a spot where the tile grout was low or missing—he felt himself being dragged lower and lower. Back to the place that had been his normal when he'd been married to Eva. When he first met with this couple about being their builder, she had said something that reminded him of Eva, and he blew it off instead of listening to his gut and turning down the job.

"I don't care if you have to stay here the entire night with zero breaks to fix it all," the woman said. "We'll be back in the morning before we head to the title company." She tossed the punch list at him. "If there's anything on there that isn't fixed, I'll plaster negative reviews of your company all over the internet and I'll tell everyone I know to stay far away." Then they both turned and strode out of the house.

Nate should have stood up for himself and his company more. But the vibes this couple had given off from the moment he'd pulled up in front of the house were just so like what he'd experienced with Eva for all those years that it had immediately taken him back to that point in his life. The point where he hadn't even known how much he was being manipulated and hadn't a clue how to fight it. He had worked hard with a good therapist and had come a long way since then, but today he was right back in the thick of it.

He immediately went to work on fixing everything on the list. He didn't have anyone he could pull from another job, so it was all on him. He wished he hadn't scheduled Donna elsewhere yesterday— she would've already been on all these details.

As he worked, he thought about how easy it would be

to blame everything on this couple. But the truth was, even if the world's kindest couple were closing on this house, he wouldn't have been okay with any of these issues. He wanted people to be thrilled with their new houses. He was the one who had over-scheduled.

So staying as long as it took to finish everything on the list was exactly what he was going to do. His integrity was riding on it.

———

By the time Nate finished everything at the home in Mountain Springs, it was already after nine, and he still had the twenty-minute drive back to Love a Latte before he could even start the painting. He was still feeling the effects of the emotional beatdown he'd gotten from the Eva-like couple during the walk-through, and couldn't quite shake it off.

If it had been any other night, he would have just texted Tory to let her know that he couldn't get to any work at her shop. She would've understood.

But just that morning, he had said that he would finish so she could open the store inside the building in the morning, and he'd seen how much joy and excitement and relief that had caused. He couldn't take that back now. That smile she had given him was all that had gotten him through the last several hours.

So, dead-tired as he was, he pulled into a parking spot in front of Love a Latte at 9:40, then dragged himself out of the truck, unlocked the front door, and turned on the lights. He made several trips to his truck to bring in the tarps, ladder, brush, roller, paint tray, and buckets of paint.

It wasn't until he was prying the lid off the top of the first gallon of paint that he saw the flowers in a vase on the counter and froze. He stayed in that same position, crouched down in front of a gallon of paint, for several moments. Tory had a few employees. Maybe the flowers belonged to one of them. He stood and carefully walked toward the flowers like they were a vicious animal devouring its prey, ready to attack anyone who got too close.

A card lay on the counter top, face-down. His hand hovered over it for a moment before he flipped it over and saw the message.

Dear Tory,
I've been thinking about you nonstop and hope you're willing to give us a second chance.
Love, Trace

This could be nothing, he told himself. Tory couldn't control Trace at all, and these may have had absolutely nothing to do with anything that she did. Logically, he knew this. He kept reminding himself of it over and over.

But it just took him back to Eva's tactics. She was always getting flowers from men. Whether they were flowers from guys she flirted with, guys she slept with, or if they were simply flowers she sent herself with a card saying it was from an admirer, he never really knew. But he did know that Eva's purpose behind the flowers was to make him jealous. She always considered jealousy an important part of a relationship, believing it would make him work harder to keep her.

Maybe right now all the negative thoughts that were filling his mind were simply because he'd just dealt with someone who was very much like Eva. Maybe if he had come in and found the flowers on any other day, they wouldn't be affecting him the way they were right now. He knew that Tory didn't still have feelings for Trace. And remembering back to that morning, he knew she had feelings for him. Those smiles, that hug, that kiss— they were much too genuine to have been faked.

But the negative voice in his head pointed out that if it had been something Tory hadn't wanted, why did she leave them here, on the counter, in plain sight, with the card right next to it, when she knew that he was coming in tonight and would see them?

No. He knew Tory. She was about as different from Eva as anyone could be. He made himself pour paint into a hand bucket, get out a paintbrush, and start doing the edging.

As he was working, though, more and more thoughts kept creeping in. Bree had also seemed very different from Eva, but in the end, she'd been so much the same. And then the words Jeigh had said to him that morning when they had been clearing away the debris from the front of the building rang in his ears. *And now you're worried that if Tory shows any attraction toward you, it's because you're her contractor.*

He had told himself plenty of times that he didn't date anyone because he was never attracted to the right people and the right people were never attracted to him. There was a reason why he'd always felt it was important to remember that—it was what saved him from things going drastically wrong in relationships.

Especially a relationship like his with Tory. It wasn't just about the two of them—there were kids involved. Kids who deserved someone who would be an amazing dad. Sure, he hung out with his niece and nephew often, but that wasn't anything like knowing how to parent kids day in and day out. He had no business even considering continuing his relationship with her.

Stop, he told himself. He could feel himself hopping on the spiral that would take him down to the place where he was when he was married to Eva. He had worked long and hard to get far from that place, and he wasn't about to go back now.

He set down his paint and brush and rooted around in his tool bag until he found his headphones. Then he found a playlist with a strong, fast beat, shoved on his headphones, and turned it up loud enough that it banished any possibility of having a thought of his own, and went back to painting.

nineteen

TORY

Tory waved at Nate from the middle of the fields at Nestled Hollow Elementary, and he jogged across the grass to meet her. Her mom had fallen a couple of days ago, so she needed Tory for longer than normal on Friday night, making a date with Nate impossible. He had been seeming down and exhausted from all the hours he had been working, so Tory had encouraged him to not work at the shop for a few days to get some extra rest.

She hadn't meant to invite Nate to more family things yet because she wasn't ready to have her kids more involved with him, but she really wanted to see him and he seemed just as anxious to see her. Trace had already told the kids that he wouldn't be able to make it to Elodie's and Aspen's soccer games, so in a moment of weakness and longing to see Nate, she talked him into skipping an hour of his Saturday afternoon work and joining them there.

She hoped that the more time that Covey spent with Nate, the more he'd get used to him being around, and the less he would be upset that she and Trace were never going to get back together.

When Nate got to where she and her kids were set up with chairs, a blanket, and half a dozen bottles of water and just as many Gatorades, he stepped close and wrapped an arm around her waist, and kissed her on the lips.

"I see you're as happy to see me as I am to see you," she said.

He smiled. "Very much." He turned to the kids. Covey sat in a chair, fidgeting with a 3-D mind-teaser puzzle, Aspen was in her soccer uniform, stretching her legs, and Elodie and Jackson both sat on the blanket in their soccer uniforms. "So, who's playing?"

"I already played," Jackson said. "And we won!"

Tory chuckled. The league didn't officially keep score, but everyone kept score unofficially anyway. So, unofficially when Jackson finished his game an hour ago, his team had *not* won, but he claimed victory in every game regardless of the score. Since her goal with having her kids play sports was to learn sportsmanlike conduct, to get exercise, to learn to work together as a team, and to work hard at getting better at something— and he got all that at every game— it was close enough to the truth.

"Elodie's and Aspen's games fell at the same time. Elodie's is on that field," Tory said, pointing at the field to her left, "and Aspen's is on that one. When this happens, we just set up in the space between the two. It usually puts us on the side of the opposing team for one of the games, but this league is chill enough that it doesn't matter."

"So which way do you face your chairs?" he asked.

"Doesn't matter," Covey said, not looking up from where he sat. "Once the game starts, she doesn't sit down at all."

"Easier to see both games that way."

More and more members of the teams arrived, and her friend Brooke and her fiancé Cole carried their chairs to where Tory was set up. That meant they were on the home team side for at least Aspen's game. As families who didn't have kids on Elodie's team started setting up their chairs in between the two fields, she knew she was on the opposing team's side for that game.

"Cole!" Nate said, and the two men put one arm around each other, slapping each other on the back. "Is Sam on Aspen's team?"

"She is," Aspen said, and the two girls ran off to meet their coach by one of the goals to warm up.

Elodie ran off to join her team, too, and Tory and Nate chatted with Cole and Brooke. It was great to see Nate relaxing and enjoying the company of others— it seemed like he hadn't had nearly enough of that lately.

The games started and Tory stood up, turning her focus from one game to the other, trying to make sure she was catching the important parts of both games and cheering at all the right spots. Nate had stood up from his chair at the same time she had, and he stood next to her on the field, switching between watching both games as well.

Aspen and Sam were both forwards, one on the left and one on the right, and were both getting a lot of time with the ball. Tory noticed that her focus was being drawn to that game more often, so she made a conscious effort to keep turning to watch Elodie's game. Elodie played defense, and the team they were playing against was tough. As the game went on, more and more the game was being played on Elodie's end of the field.

A dad from the opposing team sat not far from where she was seated, and his daughter was obviously one of the forwards that Elodie was constantly trying to guard. "Don't let her block you like that," he yelled. "Plow right through her if you have to!"

Her attention was taken back to Aspen's game as she heard the crowd start to cheer, and saw that Aspen had the ball out in front of most of the players, with only a couple of defenders between her and the goal. She got close then slowed down like she didn't quite know what to do. It was a fake, though, and it threw them off and she shot for the goal, the ball going just out of reach of the goalie. The crowd let out a cheer, Tory yelling louder than all of them. "Great shot, Aspen!"

Aspen turned toward her and pumped a fist in the air a couple of times, and she pumped her fist back. As their teams set up to kick off at midfield, Tory's attention went back to Elodie's game, where Elodie was once again up against the girl whose dad wasn't just cheering on the players like the league rules stated, but he was yelling awful things about Elodie's team. The girl got past Elodie and scored a goal. Instead of just cheering for his daughter and leaving it at that, the man yelled out, "That's right! They're killin' ya because ya all suck!"

"Hey," Tory said, just loud enough for the man to hear. "Let's take it down a notch. No one came here for a verbal beating."

"It looks like their players aren't the only ones who are pansies," the man said to everyone around, whether they wanted to listen or not. "Their parents are as well. Can't even handle a little competition."

Tory tried to calm her breathing. She could feel the Mama Bear inside her coming out, and she wanted to keep it hidden, especially since Nate was here. She tried to counter the man's negative words with a great example of how to cheer on a team and hoped that everyone else around would do the same and the man would take the hint. So far, though, it wasn't working, and the man was getting louder and meaner.

Nate reached an arm around her waist— a gesture of support that Tory was grateful for. "They're six," Nate said, not loudly, but it seemed to be purposely just loud enough for the man to hear, and she loved him for it. "You would think he would remember that. And isn't this a rec league?"

Tory nodded.

The man's daughter and Elodie both went for the ball at the same time, and Elodie got hurt, falling to the ground and grabbing her leg. Tory held her breath, hoping it wasn't anything big, and didn't breathe again until Elodie stood up. She shook her leg a few times and then stepped down on it. She seemed like she wasn't hurt too badly, but when the coach asked if she wanted to come out of the game for a minute, Elodie nodded yes.

Tory met her at the sideline and asked her if she was okay, and then led her to her chair. She rubbed Elodie's ankle and asked if she wanted to keep playing.

"I want to go back in soon. Did you see me? That girl's a really good player, and I've stopped her from making a goal tons of times!"

"Yes, you did," Nate said. "You've been playing great!"

Elodie beamed and then ran to stand by her coach. It was only a few minutes before he put her back in, but it gave Tory a chance to watch Sam make a goal in Aspen's game. She was soaking in how wonderful it felt to have Nate at her side, cheering on the kids.

She hadn't even come close to wanting to date another man before Nate came along, so she hadn't imagined how situations like this would feel. It was a blissful surprise that made her wonder if maybe she could handle being married again. Maybe it would be different this time around, and she'd get to spend her life experiencing moments like this.

The halftime whistle blew for both games, and both girls came over and guzzled Gatorade. Nate seemed to sense that both of them liked to hear about what awesome things they had done in the game so he kept piling them on, and they were thrilled at his comments.

Then, someone else's comments caught her attention, and she found herself listening to the man from the opposing team as he talked to his daughter.

"That kick to her ankle was perfect!" He gave his daughter a high five. "The wimp came right out of the game, and you were able to score. Just do that again only harder, and you might get her out for the rest of the game. If you can get where her shin guards don't cover, you'll have a better chance."

Tory's heart pumped fast, her blood heating to dangerous levels as the man spoke.

The girl said, "But I got a penalty last time when I did that."

Her dad shook his head. "Just make it look like you're going for the ball, and you won't get penalized. If she falls, you fall, too. The ref will think it was just two players going for the same ball."

Tory couldn't stand by and do nothing any longer. She stormed over to where the man was sitting. "You are teaching your daughter to injure other players so she can score a goal?!" Her voice came out like thunder and she didn't care. "These girls are *six*. What kind of a person teaches a six-year-old to cheat and injure other players?"

The man stood up. "The kind who doesn't want to raise a pansy who will come out of the game with any little injury."

He puffed out his chest, trying to seem taller and larger and more intimidating. But Mama Bear was out, and her cub was the one in danger. Tory stood to her full height. Her frame wasn't very wide, but she took a step closer to the man anyway, a fierceness pouring through her that she hoped he could see, and he took a slight step back. "Keep the game civil. Let the kids have fun and play the game."

"Or what? You're going to go cry to the ref?"

She ignored the man and kept staring at him, not lessening her intensity, not backing down. She was not going to be the first one to flinch. For several long moments, they stood face-to-face, and then the man said, "Game's starting. I don't know about you, but I want to see how my daughter does against yours." Then he took a seat.

Tory calmed herself enough to give Elodie and Aspen smiles and high-fives and sent them back to their respective fields. Inside, though, she was still shaking and fuming.

"Maybe you should tell the ref," Nate said.

Tory shook her head. "The refs are fourteen. They can't stand up to a guy like that, and I'd never ask them to. This is a casual league. It isn't set up to deal with stuff like this."

She couldn't change who this man was— only he could. It bothered her, though, to know that not only did they have to endure another half of him shouting rude things to the players and encouraging his daughter to hurt her daughter, but that he'd keep doing it to other teams the entire rest of the season.

"If you need it," Brooke said, shaking her phone, "I videoed his conversation with his daughter."

Tory's eyebrows rose. "You did?" Brooke nodded, so she said, "Text it to me." The back of the girls' jerseys had the Hungry Hamburger logo, a fast food restaurant in Mountain Springs. She looked up the restaurant's phone number on her phone, pushed to dial it, then walked away from the fields to talk.

The manager happened to be working, and once she explained what had happened and texted him the video, the manager asked to speak to the man. Tory gladly walked her phone over to him and held it out. "Phone's for you."

The man looked confused, but took the phone and barked a "Hello."

She couldn't tell what the manager on the phone was saying, but she sensed he'd had issues like this dad at a sports game for his own kid because whatever he was saying didn't encourage the man to talk back much.

When the call was over, the man shoved the phone back at Tory and then yelled for the coach to pull his daughter out for a minute. When his daughter came over to see what he wanted, he said, "Don't hurt anyone, or Hungry Hamburger won't sponsor the team anymore, and all funding will be pulled." He threw a glare in Tory's direction, and then added, "And not for just this game— for all season."

Tory was thrilled that she wouldn't have to worry about Elodie being purposely injured and that there weren't going to be any other kids in the league targeted for the rest of the season.

She was embarrassed, though. Whenever Tory went all Mama Bear— at a game or anywhere else— Trace always joked that he was just going to go pretend to be a dad for the other team, so no one would know he was married to her. Even her mom had suggested that she shouldn't do things that might intimidate people, or she wouldn't get a man.

She turned back around. "Where's Nate?"

"He got a phone call." Covey didn't look up from his toy. "He said to tell you he had to leave."

Across the fields, Tory saw Nate's retreating figure as he walked to his truck in the parking lot. She knew that going Mama Bear on someone was a trait that made her less worthy of love—she had been told it often enough. And she really tried to keep it in. She knew that her feelings got a little intense when someone she loved was in danger. But what was she supposed to do? Sit back and let her kid get targeted? She could never do that.

But it did make her wish that she hadn't asked Nate to come to this game. Later, he may laugh it off or joke about how aggressive she just was, but she knew that it didn't matter what he said about it. What mattered was how much that kind of thing turned people off.

This was, by far, not her only flaw. And the longer she dated Nate, the more things like this he'd find out about her, and the less he'd be interested in continuing to date her. The longer he went before realizing all of her flaws, the more her heart was going to be invested in him. The more her kids were going to be invested in him.

Going through her divorce with Trace had been the most difficult thing she'd ever experienced, and she knew that her heart couldn't handle going through anything like that ever again. She knew her kids couldn't do it again, either. The smart, healthy thing would be to back off now before she— or her kids— got entangled any more than they already were.

NATE

Nate spent the morning visiting each of his job sites, seeing how the work was coming along at each, taking an inventory of what each of them needed next, and checking if there were any building materials they would need soon that he hadn't already delivered to the sites. So far, his crews seemed to be holding up fairly well, considering how many hours they were all working. He hoped that held out.

Armed with a list of all the things he would need to visit the home improvement store for, he headed to his last site— the one he had been most looking forward to inspecting, and not just because he hadn't gotten his coffee yet today.

The line had a few people in it, but Tory still noticed him walk into the shop and threw him a smile. As he waited, he took another look at everything. Except for a night or two a week that he had been spending with Tory, and of course, her ban on working on it on Sundays, Nate had been spending virtually every night on it, and it was coming right along.

With only him working on it, though, and for only a few short hours a night, it wasn't coming along nearly as quickly as he was used to things progressing. But at least he'd gotten it to the point where she could run her coffee shop from actually inside the coffee shop. He added a few things to his list that he knew this job would need soon.

"Hi," Tory said as the person in front of him walked away with their coffee. Her smile was warm and washed over him like it was rain in a desert, and she reached out to his hands that were on the counter and held them, her thumb moving back and forth against the top of his hand. "I was wondering if I'd get to see you today."

"I'm just heading to Denver for some supplies and I wanted your face to be the last thing I saw before I hit the road." He wanted her face to be the last thing he saw before everything he did, but he wasn't quite sure she felt the same. For the most part, things had been going great between them. But sometimes she'd give him a look that he couldn't quite interpret, and it always left him feeling like he wasn't measuring up.

If the look she was giving him right now was all he had to go on forever, though, he would be dropping to a knee right now. Her eyes studied his like she loved what she was seeing. "How about a vanilla latte today?"

He gave her a mischievous smile. "You're anticipating my day to be rough, huh? Or is it that I already look haggard?"

She winked and then turned to the back counter to make his drink. "Or maybe it's because you agreed to come to Covey's piano recital tonight, and I know that piano recitals can sometimes require loading up on caffeine beforehand."

Nate laughed a booming laugh. "I'm looking forward to it; no extra caffeine needed."

———

Nate walked into the massive home improvement store, double-checking his list. There were plenty of construction supplies that he could get delivered to each site, but there were some things he had to come to the store for. And with an hour-long drive in each direction and the lack of time he had, he wasn't about to forget something that would require him to come back anytime soon.

He grabbed a flatbed cart, headed down one of the main aisles, and froze. There, looking at the washers and dryers, was Eva. Oh, and more of what he needed— she happened to be there with her parents.

It had been a good two years since he'd last seen Eva, and nearly three since he'd been in the same room as his ex-in-laws. He started looking for escape routes— a direction he could go and not be seen by them.

But before he'd taken his first step, Eva's mom spotted him and tapped Eva on the shoulder. Eva looked up and then her gaze found him and she waved. He closed his eyes for a short moment before heading in their direction.

Eva still looked the same as always. Her blond curls were perfectly cascading down her back, her nails perfectly manicured, and her earrings perfectly flashy and expensive. And her mom still had the same stick-straight hair that fell almost to her shoulders and the uptight expression. Her dad noticed him next, and he definitely still had the large, intimidating frame.

Why couldn't he have gotten stuck in traffic on the way here? Or had a flat tire. Or ran into a problem that delayed him at one of his sites. Or been struck by lightning. He would've taken any of them.

Instead, he was pushing his big flat cart toward a group of people that made him realize that he hadn't spent nearly enough time being grateful for not having seen them in so long.

He left his cart at the edge of a Whirlpool front loader and took the last few steps into the washer and dryer area and nodded at Eva's parents. "Mr. and Mrs. Goodrich. It's nice to see you again. Hello, Eva."

Mrs. Goodrich came forward and gave him her version of a hug, which included her placing her hands on his shoulders, like she wanted all the power of choosing how close to each other they came, then leaning slightly in. He was okay with that kind of hug coming from her because it meant he didn't have to do anything to reciprocate. "It's nice to see you, too."

Eva's dad stuck his hand toward Nate, so he reached out and shook it.

"So how are you?" Mrs. Goodrich asked. "Are you still running that little construction company of yours?"

Ignore the snide comment, he told himself.

"I heard you moved back to…" Mr. Goodrich tapped a finger on his lip. "What was the name of that place out in the sticks where you are from?"

Nate took a slow, deep breath. And then he told himself that he didn't need to try to justify anything about his life because he didn't care what these people thought of him at all.

"Nestled Hollow, and yes, I'm still running Elsmore Construction." He turned toward Eva, hoping that signaled the end of the conversation with her parents.

"Hello, Nate." She came out from behind the washer she had been checking out, holding her hand out like he was supposed to, what? Kiss it like she was royalty?

And that's when he noticed that she was pregnant. Quite far along, too. He knew he had frozen, staring at that belly with the baby growing inside, when she dropped her hand and in one fluid motion turned to wave to someone behind her by the dryers. "Honey, come to say hi to Nate."

Nate's attention flew to the man. He'd been so focused on Eva and her parents that he hadn't even noticed Declan Powers, the man who had been his and Eva's neighbor back when they were married. A lawyer, if he wasn't mistaken. Also, if he wasn't mistaken, one of the men who had sent his wife flowers during their marriage.

"You remember Nate, right, Declan?" Eva asked as the man neared.

"Of course! Nate, good to see you!" He shook Nate's hand with far too much gusto. "How the heck are you, buddy?"

They were both wearing rings. So she'd gotten remarried.

"Good. And I guess congratulations are in order," Nate said, motioning to Eva's stomach.

The man put an arm around Eva's shoulder. "Yep, and we couldn't be happier. We've got a big house, and we're ready to fill it with a bunch of little Powers kids."

"Sounds like a good reason for a new washer and dryer. It was great seeing you all again. If you'll excuse me, I've got to hurry and grab some building supplies and head back to Nestled Hollow."

He grabbed his cart and shoved it in the direction of

the heaviest thing on his list—floor tiles and bags of grout — and wished he had a demolition he needed to get back for. He could use a few hours of swinging a sledgehammer into a wall.

As he piled box after box of tiles onto his cart, he kept replaying in his mind the moment when Eva stepped out from behind that washer and he saw her pregnant belly. So she had wanted kids after all. Her hesitation really was because he wasn't good enough. Maybe if he had decided to become a lawyer instead of running his "little" construction company, she would've decided that he was good enough for her.

Not that he wanted to be good enough for her. One thing he had been grateful for all these years was finally getting away from her.

Still, it stung.

And made him question if he was good enough to be a father.

He threw a bag of mortar, a bag of grout, and the box of grout color onto the cart and then shoved it toward the plumbing aisle.

twenty-one

TORY

Tory was late getting dinner on the table, so now they were all running behind. She was scrambling to get everyone dressed nicely and time was ticking by at an insanely fast rate.

"I can't find my church shoes!" Jackson called out.

"Again? Honey, remember, you're supposed to only take them off in your bedroom so they don't get lost!"

"I did!"

"Aspen?" Tory called out as she rushed out of her bedroom, putting her heels on as she went.

"On it."

"Mom," Covey said as he raced up the stairs, panic written all over him. "I can't find my music— I've searched everywhere!"

She followed him down the stairs. "Where did you have it last?"

Covey motioned with both hands at the end table next to the front door. "I put it right here so I could grab it easily on our way out. And now it's gone! Mom, I'm not kidding you. I one hundred percent know I put it here."

"I believe you." She looked around the room, trying to see if it could've been knocked off anywhere. She heard a quiet growling and looked in the square of space where the two couches came together at the corner of the room and saw the dog chewing on the corner of it. "Nacho!" She reached down between the couches, pried it out of his mouth, and then held it up. "I'm so sorry, Covey. It's just on the corner—"

Covey let out a strangled cry as he lurched forward and grabbed the book. "Stupid dog." He quickly flipped through it.

"Is it okay?"

"There's a couple of notes missing on each page, but I think I probably have it memorized enough. As long as the pages won't stick together when I'm on stage."

"Make sure you can open each page just fine on the way there, and you'll be good." She called out, "Van's leaving in thirty seconds—grab whatever you need and get out there quickly!"

Once everyone was in the van, she raced across town to Nestled Hollow Middle School. Her life was so crazy and such a mess so much of the time. What was she doing, thinking that she could throw a relationship into the mix when she couldn't even handle everything as it was? The whole reason she had gotten dinner late to the table was because she had been texting Nate and hadn't realized how much time had passed.

She'd heard her phone buzz several times during the drive, so as everyone was getting out of the vehicle, she pulled it out of her purse. There was a text from Nate and four from Trace, all asking if she was close. Like stopping to read and respond to texts was going to make her get there more quickly. She shoved it back in her purse.

When they got into the building, Nate and Trace were both leaning against the walls on opposite sides of the wide hallway between the front office and the auditorium. Both men stood up straight when they came in. Tory bent down to tie Jackson's shoes since that little detail had somehow gotten missed.

"Should I go get us seats?" Nate asked.

Trace crouched down to tie Jackson's other shoe— something he never did— his elbows bumping into hers.

"Mom," Covey said, panicked, "these two pages keep sticking! When I'm up there and trying to flip the page, I can't use both hands, and it keeps taking both hands!"

She was still crouched, about two seconds from finishing double-knotting Jackson's shoe, but Nate stepped in. "I'll help you, buddy." He inspected the damage, then worked to pull a bit of the edge with teeth marks and mostly dried dog saliva off the book so it wouldn't keep catching. One spot caught when trying to turn the page, though, so he tried to tear it off, and with a loud *rrrriiippppp!*, the page tore a good three-fourths of the way up to the top.

The looks of horror and strangled gasps for both Covey and Nate were pretty equal.

"I am so sorry," Nate said as Covey took the book, examining the tear. Nate looked toward the auditorium. "Maybe we can see if someone has some tape somewhere." His voice trailed off as sounds of Covey's teacher welcoming everyone came through the speakers.

Tory stood next to Covey, both of them hurriedly checking the turning quality of the pages, especially the torn one, Covey looking even more stressed out, when Trace said, "You're late—you're supposed to be sitting up there already. You better run."

"Mom!" Covey said, taking two steps toward the door and then two back to her, unsure what to do and too panicked to do nothing.

"You two aren't helping," she snapped at both Nate and Trace. Then she turned to Covey, crouching down to his height, turning his shoulders toward her so he would give her his focus.

"Covey," she said in the calmest voice she could muster. "You've practiced this piece so many times; I know you know it with your eyes closed. You are going to be awesome up there. Look at me. Two deep, slow breaths." Then she breathed right along with him. "Now let's see you stand tall. Shoulders back. Fists on your hips. Good, good. Okay, now no need to rush—just walk down that aisle confidently, join the others on the front row, and go show them what you've got."

Hopefully, the kid would be able to shake off the craziness just fine. "Okay, let's get in there," she said to the others.

Nate was suddenly at her side. He reached down to entwine his hand in hers and then gave it a squeeze. She tried to take a few calming breaths herself, and then entered the dark auditorium as the kids ran ahead, Nate on her left and Trace on her right.

The kids chose a row right in the middle, and they had all gone in to grab a seat before Tory got there. Jackson was struggling to get the padded seat pulled down and staying down long enough for him to climb in it, and Aspen and Elodie sat on either side of him, leaving the three seats closest to the aisle open.

Since Covey's piano teacher was already on stage and Nate was already at her left, she motioned for him to go in first and sit next to Aspen, and then she sat next to him, leaving Trace sitting at her other side.

She let out a breath of air that accidentally came out as an annoyed huff. Just what she wanted— to be sitting between two guys who had been posturing for dominance like two alpha wolves since she had arrived and were both making things worse as they tried to claim territory.

As the first ten-year-old sat down at the piano, which was thankfully not Covey, giving him more time to recover, Elodie came over to Tory and climbed on her lap, whispering into her ear, "This is a pretty song. Isn't it so pretty? I think I want to start taking piano lessons so I can play pretty things like this. Can I start, please?"

Tory turned her head and brushed Elodie's hair away from her ear so she could whisper back as quietly as possible. "Remind me when we get home and we'll talk about it, okay?"

Elodie didn't vacate her lap after her question, though. She just maneuvered her six-year-old body, which was way too big for sitting on a lap in these chairs, until she could see, and settled in. Tory shifted herself so she could see around Elodie, and then pulled out her phone in anticipation of recording Covey's performance.

Noises and way too loud whispers for such a quiet space came from her left, and she shifted Elodie so she could look toward Aspen and Jackson. They were playing what was apparently a rousing game of rock, paper, scissors, and had completely forgotten piano recital behavior. True, she had been too frazzled and hadn't reminded them in the van on the way over what she had expected of them, but this wasn't their first recital, and they knew.

She leaned close to Nate. "Do you mind switching seats with Aspen and trying to keep Jackson quiet?"

Then Trace leaned forward and said, not even in a whisper, "Stay where you are, Nate. I've got this— I'm their dad."

Then Trace stood up and knocked into Tory's and Elodie's knees and then Nate's knees as he made his way past them and then Aspen and Jackson to sit on the other side of Jackson, causing the few dozen people in the auditorium all to turn in their seats and shoot them angry glances. Tory closed her eyes and shook her head. Then she lifted Elodie off her lap and placed her in the seat that Trace had just vacated.

Getting four kids dressed in church clothes and to the auditorium so soon after dinner was tough enough. Getting here with Nate and Trace present made things twice as difficult. This recital would be going so much more smoothly if neither of them was here.

The thought gave her a knot in her stomach. Yes, it had been a frustrating evening. But still, that didn't excuse the fact that there she was, getting annoyed at Nate to the point of snapping at him for trying to be helpful in a way that wasn't helpful when he had zero experience being a parent. She had become a parent one kid at a time, her ability as a mom growing as they grew, yet still, she got it wrong a good portion of the time.

She was alarmed to realize a thought that historically she had only aimed at Trace she was now thinking about Nate— the thought that for so long she had been so used to doing everything herself and being the one person in charge that she no longer could be a partner.

When she had gotten over the pain of Trace saying he was leaving her for someone else, when she had finally gotten to where she could be introspective and realize exactly how much of the divorce was her fault, she had realized that she had been awful at actually being a wife.

She had wondered back then if the reason she had first been drawn to Trace when she was twenty was because she could sense that when they needed to start acting like adults, he wouldn't be able to. She wondered if part of her had married him, knowing that he would take a step back and let her plow ahead, being the one adult to take charge. To be the one in control. Maybe that was what she had craved without even realizing it.

And now that she was doing the same thing with Nate, she understood all over again that it was all her. As one student finished and walked off stage then Covey walked up onto the stage, it sunk in that she must not be able to function as a co-parent, a co-adult, or a co-partner. She had to control things more than she had been willing to admit. Just like at the soccer game with the jerk of a dad, she'd needed to protect and control.

She had always taken pride in being a fully independent mom who could do everything herself. Maybe that was her fundamental flaw— that she was incapable of giving up her fierce independence and control in order to have someone to lean on.

twenty-two

NATE

After hearing Covey pound out a rhythm on the side of a wheelbarrow that day they cleaned up the destruction in front of Love a Latte, Nate should've guessed the kid would be able to play the piano this well. Still, it caught him off guard. Covey was impressive, especially for a ten-year-old.

Especially for a ten-year-old who had a page of his music torn nearly in half. Nate cursed himself for his poor choice. Having Trace here had made him feel like he needed to somehow compete— to show that he could be helpful when it came to Tory's kids. But what he had been was the furthest from helpful.

And this was just one moment. A moment that had lasted less than five minutes, and his attempts had only made the situation worse.

He glanced over at Tory as she held her phone in one hand, recording, but had her eyes glued on Covey, not the recording, her face glowing at seeing her child perform. Moments ago, he had sensed the frustration rolling off her in waves, but for this moment, she glowed.

And he got it. Whenever he wasn't daydreaming about Tory and what it might be like to have a life with her, he found himself thinking about her kids and what it would be like to be a dad to them. They were some pretty great kids and it was easy to be proud of them and to have his chest swell whenever they did something like play the piano on stage or shoot a soccer goal.

But as much as he'd love that role of dad—a role he'd been hoping to get his entire adult life— he knew that he had no clue what he was doing. Virtually no skills, no knowledge, no experience. Whenever he pictured himself as a dad, he always pictured himself being a stellar one. One who knew how to handle each situation thrown at him. One whose actions would help to raise incredible, amazing kids who would grow into incredible amazing adults.

So far, he only had flashes of experiences with it—time spent with his niece and nephew, and bits of time here and there with Tory's kids. Just enough for him to understand that he didn't know the first thing about being a dad. Which was painfully obvious when it came to Covey. With him, Nate seemed to do everything wrong.

And maybe it wasn't just about a lack of knowledge or skills or experience. Maybe Eva had been right all along in not wanting to have kids with him. Maybe he just had terrible dad instincts. And if she was right about that, maybe she was also right about him being terrible husband material.

Or maybe seeing Eva today— pregnant, no less— along with his ex-in-laws, and his ex-neighbor lawyer was messing with his mind and making him spiral. He tried to think back to how his therapist had helped him in the beginning to escape her influence, but his mind was too jumbled right now, and he just kept coming up blank.

It didn't help that Trace was sitting to his left, pulling off a covert game of rock, paper, scissors with Aspen and acting like a pro at the whole dad thing.

It also didn't help that the energy coming off Tory that had been frustration at the beginning turned to elation during Covey's performance, and was something entirely different now that he was done performing. He glanced at her face to see if he could guess what she was thinking or feeling, but he couldn't figure it out. All he knew was that it wasn't good.

When the last kid finished playing, they all came up on stage for their final bows and the instructor thanked everyone for coming and invited them to the lobby for cookies. Covey came down from the stage, and then ran up the aisle and joined them.

"Did you see?" he said to Tory, holding out his music. "I got all the pages turned, even the ripped one, which was difficult! And there was only that one tiny part that I messed up on, but I think I covered it up pretty well."

"You sure did," she said. "You were amazing."

"It was beautiful," Nate added, and Covey actually beamed.

But then Trace came up between them and started playfully punching him in the shoulder. "You knocked their socks off, kiddo! I think this deserves some kind of celebration. Want to go out for ice cream with your dad?"

Nate nearly rolled his eyes at how pointedly Trace said the word "dad." This was a turf war, and Nate was losing badly. And maybe he should. Maybe a loss here would prevent a much huger loss later on when the stakes were much higher.

After all the kids ran up to the refreshment table and each grabbed a cookie, Nate stepped close to Tory and said, "Can we talk for a minute?"

Tory studied him for a small moment, but he couldn't read her expression. Then she reached into her purse and pulled out her keys. "Um, Trace, can you do me a favor?" Trace's attention perked up, and Nate was pretty sure that he would've done anything she asked at that moment. She held out her keys. "Do you mind getting the kids in the van for me and waiting there with them until I come out? Kids, I'll be out in just a couple of minutes, okay?"

She motioned with her head at the end of the hall where it turned. Nate nodded and caught one last glimpse of Trace, who was watching him with a smug look on his face.

They rounded the corner at the end of the hall and Tory collapsed against the wall across from the middle school girls' bathroom, looking exhausted. She rubbed her hands over her face, and Nate wanted to reach out and lay his hand on her cheek and tell her that everything would be okay. But he wasn't sure it was.

"I think we should probably admit that it's time to break up," he said.

She looked up, a moment of shock and hesitation crossing her features.

He shook his head. "I can't do this. I don't know how to do this. I'm sorry. I wish things were different."

Tory nodded. "I wish things were different, too. I am just too much of a mess, my life's too much of a mess, and things with my kids are just too complicated."

The expression on her face was so sad and broken and he hated that he had caused it. He wanted to wrap his arms around her and kiss her temple and take every single bit of her hurt away. He wanted to fix more than her coffee shop— he wanted to be there to fix anything that made her sad throughout her life. He wanted to hold her and comfort her and laugh with her and cry with her and be by her side through tough times and hope and dream and make plans with her. He wanted to be with her through everything.

But he was not making things in her life better; he was making things harder. And he had fallen so deeply, crazily, hopelessly in love with this woman that he couldn't continue to do that to her.

So he gave a single nod, took a steadying breath, and said, "I understand."

Then he quickly turned back the way they had come and left so she wouldn't have to witness what losing her was doing to him.

twenty-three

TORY

Tory used all the strength she had in her to not walk out of the middle school with tears in her eyes. Still, Trace had been married to her for a decade, so it wasn't hard for him to guess what had happened. And he'd seemed a little too giddy about it.

Trace had wanted a "family" outing to get ice cream, but Tory gave a firm no. The kids had already eaten cookies, after all, and it was a school night. The celebration would have to wait until he had them on Friday night. They were all good reasons, but the real one was that moment with Nate had practically torn her heart out of her chest and she was struggling to hold herself together.

Tory had been feeling like they should break up all night and Nate had obviously agreed. But even if he did agree that it was for the best, it still hurt him. The look on his face when they'd rounded that corner to get some privacy kept playing through her mind. That haunted, defeated look. It had made her want to reach out to him, and it had taken all of her willpower not to.

And that look of tender caring on his face. Nate was an incredible guy, and she wished she could be everything he deserved her to be.

Once they arrived home, she told the kids they could stay up thirty minutes longer than normal and watch a TV show together if they ran and got their pajamas on quickly. Part of her wanted them to go to bed soon so she could let her emotions have free rein. But a bigger part wanted them there with her so she wouldn't be alone.

So she chose an animated TV show with zero romance, about a mother polar bear who was trying to keep her cubs safe while teaching them to hunt for food, while the cubs had plenty of antics and got themselves into one amusing bind after another. Her kids came racing into the room, not realizing what had gone on in the school after they had left, and all snuggled up to her on the couch. She put her arms around them as they lay against her sides and on her lap and held them close, soaking in their goodness and love and warmth for as long as she could.

When the show finished, she got them all into bed. She was mentally exhausted and probably should've gone to bed, too, but her heart was hurting too much to be alone, closed up in a room where the walls were pushing in on her. So she opened the blinds to the patio so the kids could see her if they got out of bed for something and came looking for her, then she walked out onto the patio and into the cool evening air.

She closed her eyes and breathed in the mountain air deeply, the breeze just cool enough to spread chills across her arms. As if her body was saying that it had held in her emotions as long as it could, with her exhale came sobbing tears.

Her mind went back to all the moments they had shared over the past six weeks. From all the times when she had stopped in to Love a Latte in the evenings when he was working just to see him, to all his early morning trips to the shop for coffee, to all the ways in which he had shown support for her and her kids, to stolen kisses when the kids weren't looking, to kisses across the counter at Love a Latte, to times when he would squeeze her hand or touch her shoulder or kiss her knuckles or run his fingertips down her arms, to all the ways he selflessly helped her.

She loved Nate, she was sure of it. She loved every little thing about him. His kindness, the way he served others, his booming laugh, his hopefulness, his energy, his heart. She even loved all the things she didn't know about him yet.

A dozen years ago, she had fallen in love with Trace

just as quickly and just as fully. Her capacity to love had grown so immensely since then, though, that her love for Nate felt vastly bigger, broader, and more expansive than even the early days with Trace.

Which made this fall so much greater than anything she had experienced. Tory sunk into a patio chair and let the sadness of losing such a good man wash completely over her.

NATE

Nate knocked on Beckett's front door, and a moment later, his brother opened it.

"Nate! To what do we owe this sur— Dude, what happened to you?" Beckett paused a beat, then said, "Oh no. Tory?"

Nate nodded. "Can I borrow your dog?"

Beckett's eyebrows came together. "Borrow? My dog?"

"Just for a little while. My apartment is too empty. I can't go there right now." He had stopped home just long enough to change out of his dress clothes and into jeans and a t-shirt, and just being there that long had been too much.

Beckett opened the door wider and stepped out of the way, motioning to the inside of his house. "Don't be alone. Come hang out with us."

Casey and Chantele were running all over the house, squealing in delight as Kimberly chased after them, trying to get them into pajamas. He shook his head. He couldn't stay with Beckett and be right in the middle of everything he wanted but would likely never have.

Beckett seemed to understand well enough without any more of an explanation, gave him a nod, then turned and called his dog. A moment later, he returned with the golden retriever and handed him the leash.

Nate crouched down and rubbed Sunny's face and under her collar, then took the leash. "Thanks, Beckett. I'll bring her back before it gets too late."

He led Sunny to his truck and let her hop in the cab next to him, then drove to the lake and pulled into a parking spot. The night was a little chilly, so he grabbed a flannel shirt from the passenger's side and put it on over his t-shirt. Then he got out of the cab and Sunny jumped down after him.

"Should we go for a walk around the lake?" he asked her.

The dog barked what Nate was sure was a yes, since the dog always seemed to be up for everything. So Nate held her leash and made his way down to the lake path.

The night was clear, so a brilliant swath of stars shone overhead and reflected on the lake, slight ripples on the water scattering them. Off in the distance, crickets chirped for the first time he'd heard this season. He took a deep breath of the night air, hoping that the chill would help to clear his foggy mind, yet also worried that the chill would help clear his foggy mind because it might make the evening even more painful.

Everything with Tory had been like a dream. He hadn't realized how dim his life had been until Tory came along and shone a light on his world. He had been basking in it so much that he'd ignored the little voice that told him it was too good to last.

As he rounded the top part of the lake, Sunny must have seen a squirrel or a chipmunk, because she raced ahead, nearly pulling the leash out of Nate's hand, barking repeatedly. "No, Sunny. Come on; let's keep walking."

The dog fell into line beside him, and Nate reached a hand down and petted her back. He wasn't looking for someone to talk to, but the dog's presence made him feel like he wasn't alone, and he desperately needed that right now.

When he got around to the back side of the lake, all the emotions that had been building up hit him in full force. He sank into a nearby bench, staring straight up at the night sky, trying to keep from falling apart. When he had first seen the destruction the massive tree had done to Tory's building, he hadn't even begun to guess that was exactly what his heart was going to feel like six weeks later.

twenty-five

TORY

Tory looked up from the lobby of Love a Latte when Alete walked in, then finished wiping off one of the tables.

"Look at that," Alete said, spreading her arms wide. "An empty shop—a rare occurrence."

"Today hasn't been super busy, especially for a Monday."

Alete motioned at Tory, her hand fluttering extra when she aimed it toward Tory's face. "Maybe it's because of all that moping and sadness that's emanating from you. It's so strong; it's even bursting out of the building. Seriously, it nearly knocked me down when I opened the door to come in."

"Ha ha," Tory said and headed back to the counter. "I assume you came in for some coffee?"

Alete put her hand on Tory's arm, stopping her, so Tory turned around. "No, I came in to check on my friend." They both leaned against the front of the counter.

"I'm okay," Tory said.

Alete looked her up and down. "Yeah, I can see that. It's been completely obvious over the past four days." She rolled her eyes. "Okay, Tory, I'm going to lay it out straight for you. You, Tory Beckstead, don't get this sullen over the ending of something that should've ended. That should be a major clue that maybe you two made a wrong choice in breaking up."

"It was the right choice. Maybe I'm this sullen because of how much I wish that I could be the kind of person that Nate deserves in his life. But I'm not. Maybe someday I'll be good enough, but right now I'm just not."

"Wow." Alete turned so that her backside was against the counter, her arms crossed, staring out aimlessly at the lobby. "I knew that your divorce had beaten you down, but I had no idea that it had beaten you down this badly. From the outside, you just always seem so independent and put together."

There was that word again. "Yep, independent. And I've decided that it's a good thing I'm so fiercely independent—it's going to come in handy for my life spent alone."

Alete turned to Tory, grabbing her shoulders. "Tory! This. Is. Not. You." A little shake accompanied each word.

"You are not the girl who mopes. You are the girl who goes out and fights. That's who you are. Is Nate a good guy?"

Tory nodded. "The best."

"Then why are you not out fighting for him?"

Tory shook her head and headed off behind the counter, where Alete's words wouldn't be hitting her straight on. She picked up a rag and started wiping the counter. "Because he deserves a woman who's not constantly trying to control chaos, pretending she's got it all together, and that, very sadly, is not me."

Alete reached out across the counter and grabbed her arms by the elbows. "He *deserves* a woman who will love him unconditionally, not a woman who's perfect. I wish that when you looked into the mirror, you could see what the rest of us see. You are amazing, Tory, and every single guy in the world would be lucky to have you in their life. Nate Elsmore, specifically, would be thrilled."

A single tear escaped Tory's eye and rolled down her cheek, her vision blurry from the ones that hadn't spilled out.

"Now you," Alete said, releasing Tory's arms and slapping her hands down on the countertop, "stop moping and everything else that is un-Tory-like. Stand tall, summon your inner Tory, and go out and fight for that man!"

A breath came out of Tory that was part sob, mostly a laugh, and she grabbed a napkin from the counter and dabbed at her eyes. "Thank you. I needed a little bit of Alete in my life today."

Once Alete left, Tory looked around the shop she had owned for the past eight years. Six weeks ago, she had been devastated when everything literally came crashing down. Now, though, everything was slowly coming back together.

Even over the past four days since they had broken up, Tory still came to work each morning and saw that Nate had been there the night before, getting it even closer to being finished. The section of floor that used to be bare plywood now was tiled in a pattern that he had run around the two other outside edges of the store. The walls were new and painted and blended seamlessly into the existing walls. Trim was up, too, but not painted yet.

He had even taken the time to fix the gate that led behind the counter, so now she could just bump into it as she walked behind the counter and it would swing open on its own—no need to lift up on it with her foot first to keep it from catching. She couldn't believe he had remembered about it, or that he'd taken the time to fix it when there were so many other things to do.

Day after day as Nate worked, the building that had been so broken was being healed. Unlike the speed at which that tree had come down on her building, Tory's heart had been breaking slowly over so many years that she hadn't realized just how broken it was. As she stared at her building, she couldn't help but see the metaphor in it, like a giant gift from God, yelling at her to see and finally understand.

Could Nate help her heart to heal just like he was helping her building to heal? It would require her to be vulnerable in ways that she had long ago forced herself to not be. Being strong and tough had gotten her through everything. Was it even possible for her to pull back the shields and let him in? Just the thought of it terrified her.

But so had that ropes course. She had pulled back the shields then, and Nate had proven that he would protect her heart even when it was exposed.

Still, though, the fear that he would run if she let him see all of her deficiencies was strong. And that grip she had on her shields was every bit as strong.

NATE

Nate hurried to finish up the trim he was cutting with his crew, and then left them working and hopped into his truck. He'd gotten a text from Beckett saying there was a problem at the site where he was working, and he needed Nate to come to deal with it.

Please don't be a water leak, he thought as he pulled up to the home Beckett was at. Everything was sheetrocked and painted and just waiting for flooring. He walked into the house and called Beckett's name, the sound echoing through the house.

"Back here," Beckett said, so Nate headed in the direction of his voice.

He walked into the room Beckett was in, and saw that Jeigh, his mom, and his dad were all there, too, all sitting on 5-gallon buckets and crates of flooring.

"Oh," Nate said, realization dawning on him. "*I'm* the problem. An intervention, huh?"

"Well," Beckett said, giving him a hearty pat on the back, "walk around here like a shell of yourself for long enough and you've got to expect it."

Jeigh grinned. "I wanted to hang a big 'Welcome to your intervention' banner, but Mom thought it would be tacky."

His mom hid a smile and shook her head.

"Have a seat," Beckett said, motioning to a stack of hardwood flooring facing the four of them.

Nate sat down. He could tell by the looks on their faces that he was going to need it.

"We get that you like Tory," his dad said. "Tell us: do you love her?"

"I do," Nate said without hesitation.

His dad nodded. "We all like her— she's an easy girl to like. Tell us why you love her. What is it about her?"

Good. They were starting easy. He hoped all their questions would be like this. "She's incredible. She has this fire burning inside of her— a passion for everyone she loves. And she isn't afraid to stick up for anyone if something isn't right.

"You should have seen her daughters' soccer game a couple of Saturdays ago. This dad was a real tool and was trying to get his daughter to hurt Tory's daughter so she could score a goal. Tory went right up to the guy to get him to stop. The guy was easily twice her weight, yet she didn't even so much as flinch!

"Seriously, the guy looked like he was a pro at intimidation, but when Tory wouldn't back down, I saw this flash in his eyes that showed he was the one intimidated.

"I probably should've stepped in and helped more, but instead, I was just so awed by her willingness to face someone like that to make things right for her kid that I just stood back like an idiot with my jaw dropped until I got a call from a site and had to leave. I wish you could've been there.

"And then I took her on a ropes course, not knowing she was deathly afraid of heights, and you should've seen the determination she showed to get past it." He shook his head. "She's the strongest woman I've ever met. It doesn't matter how hard or scary something is; she's unstoppable. It's like her sense of right and wrong just forces her to take action.

"But it's not like she's just a fighter or anything. I've seen her just as quickly wrap a hurt kid in her arms, share a comforting word or touch, and encourage people. Her soft side is every bit as impressive. There's a reason why Love a Latte is the heart of Nestled Hollow— she cares about people, and she isn't afraid to show it. Plus, she's fun, has a great sense of humor, and is willing to try new things."

He shook his head. He could go on and on all day, but he suddenly realized that he'd probably been rambling for much longer than they had intended when they asked that question.

"Nate," Jeigh said, her arms outstretched like he was a game show prize and she was showing him to the audience. "Look at you— you're glowing!"

He glanced down, embarrassed.

"Remember when you first started dating Eva and I was eighteen and I said that I hoped that one day I would find a love like you had with Eva? I was wrong. I was so, so wrong. *This* is the kind of love I want. The kind that will make some guy glow like that just *talking* about me. Nate, my whole life I've never seen you glow like this."

"Not just now," his mom said. "You've been glowing the past six weeks."

They all nodded.

"So why aren't you going after her?" Beckett asked.

Nate shrugged the elated feeling that had overcome him while talking about her leaving the moment he thought about their breakup. The words were embarrassing, and he didn't want to say them. One glance at the faces of his family told him that they weren't going anywhere until he did, though. So he took a deep breath, and in a moment of boldness, said, "Because I wouldn't be a good enough dad to her kids."

"Did she tell you that?" his dad asked.

"Not in so many words."

Jeigh stood up. "Do you remember what your therapist told you to do at the beginning, right after getting divorced?"

"No." His head had been such a swirling, jumbled mess of fear and doubts and unsettling chaos that he had trouble thinking at all, let alone being able to figure a way out of the murky haze. He had desperately been searching for an answer to what to do but hadn't found it yet.

"Gratitude," Jeigh said. "When the Poor Me's come a knocking, it's the quickest way to block 'em, remember? It's what will get you out of your own head and out of your own sorrows. I've been using it ever since you told me about it, and it works every time."

Gratitude. He knew this. How had he forgotten? How had he gotten out of the habit? Maybe all of his gratitude had been focused on how grateful he was for Tory for so many weeks that it had become natural, so he'd forgotten about showing gratitude for everything else.

"So let's hear it, Son," his dad said. "Start listing off things you're grateful for."

He could do this. "Okay, I'm grateful for a busy construction season. I'm grateful that it allows me to easily be able to pay my crew what they're worth. I'm grateful we haven't had rain at times when it would've been destructive at some of the sites or slowed things down. I'm grateful that I've somehow still had the energy to work on Love a Latte after work. I'm grateful I'm living back in Nestled Hollow. I'm grateful for Tory and how much I've grown just by being around her."

He smiled at his family. "And I'm grateful for family who will show up to pull me out of a damaging funk." It was amazing to him how drastic and immediate the change in his mind was, and how fully things changed from discouragement and despair to hopefulness, happiness, confidence, and peace.

They must have been able to see the change in him, because Beckett said, "Okay, so now tell us— what would your therapist say about your breakup?"

Nate thought for a moment, considering what had happened and how she would have responded if he were in her office right now. "She would probably say that I was self-destructing because I didn't believe I deserved someone as amazing as Tory."

"We're here to tell you that you do, Son." His dad put his hand on Nate's mom's. "We've known it your whole life and we've just been waiting for you to find her. Now tell me, do you *want* to be a good dad to her kids?"

"I do! They're incredible. They deserve the best kind of dad there is. I just don't think I can be that great dad, no matter how much I wish I could."

"The desire to be a great dad and the willingness to work at it is all you need. It won't be easy, but the rest will come as long as you've got that."

He wanted to be a phenomenal dad and he was willing to work at it harder than he'd worked at anything in his life. Could that be enough? "You really think I can do it? Be a great dad?"

"Yes!" all four of them said at the same time. He looked at each one of their faces.

Then he stood up. He wanted to do something—anything—to convince Tory to give their relationship another chance. To give him another chance. And he wanted to do it right now. He took a few pacing steps. "What do I do? How do I convince her?"

They were all silent for a moment, and then Nate's mom spoke up. "Make her dinner. Tonight. Surprise her with it. It's the end-of-the-school-year Student Showcase at the elementary. I remember the one year that all three of you were in elementary and doing the showcase, and that night was crazy stressful. She has four kids, and she's doing it alone. Trust me; take her a homemade meal for her and her family. Lift that one thing off her list for her."

Nate nodded, wrapped his family in a quick group hug, and then took off out of the house running.

twenty-seven

TORY

Last May, Tory swore that this May she was going to be much more on top of the Student Showcase. Everyone's projects were going to be done ahead of time, she was going to make dinner the night before and have it ready to slip into the oven, and they were all going to be twiddling their thumbs waiting for 7:00 to come around.

But this year things weren't working out quite as planned. If she thought that dating Nate had distracted her and made it more difficult to stay on top of everything, it was nothing compared to how distracted and difficult nursing a broken heart was.

Over the weekend, she had managed to help Jackson finish his project, a display board with all the words he could sight-read, and Elodie was close to finishing hers, a chapter book that she wrote and illustrated herself, consisting of a bunch of copy paper folded in half and stapled along the fold. She'd helped Aspen and Covey finish big parts of theirs, but they had run out of time before completing them.

From the moment they'd all gotten home, they had been scrambling to finish Aspen's cardboard and paper-mâché topographical map of the state of Colorado and Covey's George Washington costume, complete with his own fancy hand-lettered copy of the preamble to the constitution on paper they had "aged" and a memorization of the preamble.

And now it was nearing six o'clock, the projects weren't finished, and she hadn't even begun to think about what to feed everyone for dinner, let alone make it.

All of Aspen's paper-mâché mountains had dried well overnight, but it had taken her forever today to get the entire thing painted brown, and then to dry so she could do the next step. She had Tory's laptop open on the table, looking at the satellite view of the state, trying to paint it as realistic to how it was today as possible, including which mountains would still have snow at the tops and which would be mostly green.

"Elodie, what are you doing?" she asked when Elodie opened the pantry door.

"Getting peanut butter."

"Aaaa! Get off!" Aspen yelled as the cat leaped up onto

the table, landing right in the middle of her paper plate full of brown and green and white paint blobs.

"Cleopatrick!" Tory shouted as she lunged for the cat, but it raced off too quickly to grab, leaving brown and green and white paw prints across the table and the floor, all the way to the family room carpet.

She had just grabbed a rag and was running it under water in the kitchen sink when she heard a thud, then the sound of hundreds of items hitting the floor. She spun around to see Jackson standing in the pantry, a box of cornflakes at his feet, and the entire contents of the box spread out across a ten-foot swath of the kitchen floor.

"I'm okay," he said, hands out, like he must've been worried that he was going to take a tumble as much as the box had. "The cereal isn't, though."

"Grab the broom," Tory said and tried to shoo away the dog, who had come into the kitchen at the sound and decided to romp around in the mess like it was a pile of leaves.

Covey walked into the room, panicked. "Mom, help! I glued my wig on crooked!"

"You *glued* it on? Covey! Why?" She raced toward him and the George Washington wig that she had ordered online a week ago that had arrived looking more like an elderly woman's wig than George Washington's style with the ends curled up.

"I thought you were supposed to glue wigs on. How else are they supposed to stay when you move around?"

She tested the corners of the wig, but he hadn't just put glue around the edges—the entire thing was stuck to all of his own hair so tightly that she could barely adjust it.

"Aspen, honey," she called over her shoulder, "how's that coming? Are you about done with painting?"

"You can't rush a masterpiece, Mom."

"Maybe, but that clock can. Take a look at it—if you don't hurry, your masterpiece will have to be unfinished at the showcase." Then she turned back to Covey. "Maybe we can hold down these side parts with bobby pins so it lays a little flatter, then, I don't know, curl this one side up more so it ends at the same place as the other side and looks straight. Go get the rest of your costume on, then we'll see what we can do."

She went back into the kitchen and finished tearing the wrapper off the rest of the broken blue crayons and tossed them in a paper cup. "Aspen, I'm putting these in the microwave right now. You have until they've finished melting to be done with the painting because we need to get the rivers and lakes on there if you want to still add the glitter and write the words."

"Mom. I'm going as fast as I can, so you trying to rush me is just making me stressed. It's not making me go faster."

"Jackson!" Tory called out, stepping over the cornflake

mess. "You haven't finished cleaning up your mess!" She shook her head. How did she let this day get so chaotic?

"I'm busy for just a minute, then I'll finish," he called out from the vicinity of the bathroom just off the family room.

Tory pulled the cup out of the microwave and stirred it with a Popsicle stick. "Okay, it looks like this is ready."

"I'm dressed," Covey said. "Can you help me with my hair?"

"In a minute," Tory said, jiggling the mouse on her laptop to bring the screen up again so they could see the rivers. She pinched one side of the paper cup, making a spout to pour from. "Okay, these are all the blue crayons we have, so you might want to start with the most important rivers and lakes."

"Like our lake!" Aspen said, pouring enough of the melted crayon on their little mountain town to drown them all and probably Mountain Springs as well.

Tory zoomed in on the map to get more of the rivers and lakes, trying to help Aspen figure out where on her map they would be and ignoring the fact that Nacho was still romping around in the cornflakes. "Elodie! You need to come and finish making your chapter book quickly! And Jackson—this cornflake mess!"

"We'll be right up!"

"And that's all!" Aspen said, slamming the cup down on the table triumphantly. "Now for the glitter."

The gold glitter was supposed to represent all the lights that show from a satellite view of the state at night. One little speck of glitter for each home or business. So Tory zoomed out on the map to show where the biggest cities were as Aspen spread some glue around Denver with her finger, and then popped the top off the bottle of glitter.

She was just about to sprinkle some on top when Nacho suddenly was done with the cornflakes and had an intense need to get to the family room quickly. He raced under the table to take the shortest path, knocking right into Aspen's legs in the process, making her lurch forward.

For a small moment, Tory and Aspen held their breaths, frozen, as glitter burst out of the bottle in a giant cloud of shimmering gold, all across the still wet paint, melted crayon, wet glue, and all across the shirts that both Tory and Aspen had planned to wear.

"Nacho!" Aspen shouted. "Why did you have to be such a jerk? Look at this! It's not brushing off! What do I do, Mom? It looks like four million people just moved into the mountains and are even living in the lakes and rivers! It's like a super bumpy New York City!"

"I don't know, honey. Um, try to tip it on its side and shake some off. Or maybe we can paint over some of it." She glanced at the clock and then rubbed her forehead with her fingertips. Thirty minutes. Thirty minutes was all she had to fix this mess, get everyone's stuff together, feed everyone, drive to the school, park, and get their projects inside. If she survived this night, it was going to be a miracle.

Then the sound of Nacho's paws scrabbling across the bathroom floor and giggling and squealing from Elodie and Jackson reached her ears, and dread hit her. She raced into the family room, headed for the bathroom, and saw Jackson lying on the floor, Nacho licking his face.

"What's going on in here?"

Jackson quickly sat up, pushing the dog off him, and turned to look at her.

"What is that on your face?" Then she noticed Elodie, smiling an excited but guilty smile, with a half-empty jar of peanut butter beside her. "Is that… peanut butter on your face? What in the world?"

Elodie shrugged. "Covey told me that dogs like peanut butter, so I decided to test it, just like a scientist would. And he did like it!"

"So then I put my fingers in the peanut butter," Jackson said, "to see if he would lick it right off my fingers and he did, Mama! He licked it *from my fingers.*"

"So then," Elodie said, dragging out the word, "we figured that if we were going to be real scientists, then we also needed to test to see if a dog would lick peanut butter right off a human kid's face. Jackson volunteered—" Jackson grinned, showing all of his teeth like he was so proud of himself, "—and I did the work of spreading peanut butter *all* over his face." She waved both of her hands as proof.

"And did you see Nacho, Mom? He was licking it right off me!"

Nacho was still trying to get to Jackson's face, all while Tory's stress level was rising and the clock was winding down. "You decided to test this *now?*" She took a few quick breaths like she was preparing to go into the fray. "Okay, we need to get you two cleaned up quickly! And Elodie, you still need to finish coloring your book!"

Tory was just reaching a hand out to pull Jackson to his feet when a strangled sound came from behind her. She spun to see Covey, a look of horror on his face, a curling iron in his hand. "Mom, you were busy so I tried to curl the side up myself, and it all melted to the curling iron!"

"Covey, the wig is plastic— you can't curl it with the curling iron!"

"Well, *now* I know! Two minutes ago, I didn't."

The doorbell rang, and Tory ran both hands down her face. Every one of her kids' friends would all be heading to the Student Showcase right about now, so it had to be a solicitor. *Great.* She went into the living room and opened the door, ready to give whoever it was an earful for soliciting when there was a "No soliciting" sign on her door, but instead saw Nate, a metal pan of something in his hands.

She closed her eyes, hoping this was all some awful

nightmare. But he still stood there when she opened them again.

"Hi," he said tentatively. "Can I come in?"

She looked down at her glitter-covered shirt and glanced behind her at a kid with a peanut butter-covered face, one with peanut butter-covered hands, one covered in glitter with splotches of brown, green, and white paint all over her, and one in a George Washington costume minus the curl on one side, all standing on a bed of pulverized corn flakes sparkling with glitter, half-finished projects scattered all around. Every single one of their little pieces of evidence showed exactly how much she didn't have it all together.

Her first instinct was to shut the door hard and fast. After a moment's hesitation, though, she stood tall, shoulders back, summoned her inner Tory just like Alete had told her to do, and released the grip on the shields she had guarding her heart. Then, hands shaking and heart thumping, she opened the door fully and let Nate see all of her imperfections.

twenty-eight

NATE

Nate walked into Tory's house and glanced around. His mom hadn't been joking when she'd said that Student Showcase night with four kids would be stressful.

"So, uh, what brought you here tonight?"

"I was hoping to talk to you."

"Well," she said, motioning to the chaos all around, "as you can see, now's not the best time."

"Now, see, I think that's where you're wrong," he said, walking through the living room and into the kitchen, setting the pan on the table. "From where I'm standing, it looks like you could use some help, and 'Help' is my middle name."

"It is?" Elodie asked.

"Nate—" Tory said.

But before she had a chance to continue, he said, "Have you guys eaten?"

All the kids shook their heads, so he took the paper plates he had stacked on top of the pan and handed one out to each kid. After a glance at the projects on the table and the mess on the floor, he picked up the pan and said, "Come on, let's get you guys out on the patio."

Once they were all outside, he asked if they liked tacos, and Jackson shouted, "We love tacos!" So Nate took the foil off the top of the pan and passed tacos out to all of them. Then he headed back inside to talk to Tory.

"You made them dinner?" she said, with what he was pretty sure was a tone of disbelief and awe.

He made a mental note to thank his mom for the suggestion that brought that kind of reaction from Tory, and to his sister-in-law, Kimberly, for suggesting tacos as possibly the most mess-free, portable, universally pleasing food option. "I made some for you, too." He set the pan on the table.

Tory glanced around the room, an embarrassed look on her face, and then he saw her eyes dart to the clock on the stove. He knew he didn't have much time.

He took a step closer to her. "I know I said we should stop seeing each other, and I think you felt the same way. But I'm hoping that I can convince you to change your mind." He took a slow, deep breath, hoping he would be able to get out everything he was feeling. "Tory, I love you.

I love all of you. I love the way you care. I love the way you put family before everything. I love your fierceness. I love your softness."

He took a step closer so they were only a foot apart. "I love your determination and your drive and your passion. I love how unstoppable you are." Tears spilled over her eyes and streamed down her face, but he didn't stop. "I love your smile. I love your laugh. I love your eyes and the fire and the concern behind them."

He reached up and cradled her face in his hands, brushing his thumbs on her cheeks to wipe away her tears. "I love that you face things fearlessly. I love that you come out the other side of any struggle stronger and better. I love the way you work. I love the way you play. I love the kind of mother that you are.

"And I love the way you love. Tory, I've never met anyone more incredible than you, and I want nothing more than to be by your side all my life. I want all of it, Tory. Not just the fun times at festivals or games— I want *all* of it. All the hard parts, all the boring parts, all the messy parts, all the peanut butter, glitter, cornflake parts, and even all the homework parts. And I will gladly spend my whole life learning how to be the best husband and the best dad there is."

Tory batted away a stray tear and studied him, her eyes searching his. Then she reached forward, placing her hands on the sides of his face, pulling him forward, and pressing her lips against his. Her kiss was urgent and bold and determined and vulnerable, and with each movement of her lips against his, he knew that she was pouring every bit of who she was into it.

She pulled away slightly, touching her forehead to his, and whispered, "I love you too, Nate. More than I ever thought I could."

Then she was kissing him again, this time softer and sweeter, her lips pushing and tugging at his. He dropped his hands to the small of her back, pulling her closer as heat spread through his chest, his heart quickening and pounding. When she released the kiss this time, she leaned her head on his shoulder, and he brought a hand up to stroke her hair, hugging her tight.

After a few moments of basking in the feeling of her head against him, her body pressed against his, he loosened the hug and snuck a glance outside to see that the kids were almost finished, and then kissed her on her temple. "You go get ready— I'll get the kids cleaned up."

She gave him a smile full of gratitude and then hurried up the stairs. Nate searched the kitchen until he found where the washcloths were, then got three of them wet, wrung them out, then took them outside and handed one to Aspen, one to Elodie, and went to work using the third one to wash the peanut butter off Jackson's face, hair, and neck.

"All right," he said to the kids, "what things still need to happen before we can leave?"

———

By the time Tory came back down the stairs a few minutes later, wearing a blouse not covered in glitter and the tears washed off her face, Nate had the kids cleaned up, Elodie was finishing coloring the last page of her book, he had trimmed the melted edges of Covey's wig, he and Aspen had come up with a plan, and Jackson had found his shoes.

He had hoped to get the cornflake mess cleaned up, too, but Tory had been faster than he had guessed. Which was good, because they were running out of time quickly.

"Everyone grab your projects and hop in the van," Tory said. "Let's skedaddle!"

"Grab a taco," Nate said. "I'll drive so you can eat."

She tossed him her keys, then grabbed two and put them on a paper plate. As they were driving away, Tory asked Aspen if she was able to fix her project, then she bit into a taco. Either he made tacos that were so good they were even heavenly when they were mostly cold, or she hadn't taken a chance to eat anything for hours.

"Nope, but Nate helped me come up with a plan. Instead of this map being Colorado right now, it's the Colorado of the future. This is a representation of how many people will be living here when they all realize how awesome it is to live in these mountains. They'll all figure out how great our lakes and rivers are, too, and build floating houses on them."

Nate chuckled at Aspen's enthusiasm for the new plan. These kids were nothing if not resilient.

"How about you, Covey?" Tory asked. "Are you good to go?"

"Yep! You know, Washington was a general before he was president, and he always went out to battle at the front of his men. Bullets were constantly whizzing right past him, but none of them ever hit him. This," he said, making a whooshing sound as he brushed his hand along the burned-off part, "is where one of those bullets whizzed by him so closely it shaved his hair clean off his head."

Nate could feel Tory's gaze on him, so he glanced over as he stopped at a stop sign.

She reached a hand out and placed it on his bicep. "Thank you," she said. "Truly. For everything—for being you." And he could tell that she really meant it.

Tory gathered Covey, Aspen, Elodie, and Jackson around Nate's birthday cake and spread the candles on the table. All four kids pressed the candles into the cake, each proud of where they had placed theirs. They looked up at her with questioning faces, and she said, "It looks exactly right."

She handed a fireplace lighter to Covey and said, "Help me light it," then grabbed the other one herself and together they lit them all.

Tory glanced into the family room, where she could see Nate sitting on the couch, making faces at their newborn baby Mason, and a rush of love for this man washed over her. She glanced down at her ring finger— a finger that, after her divorce, she had figured would stay bare for a very, very long time, if not forever. And now it held a ring that Nate had chosen, and nothing had ever felt so perfect on her hand.

They lit the last of the candles and she picked up the cake and slowly walked it into the family room, careful to not let any of the candles blow out. As they reached the room, they all started singing.

"Happy birthday to you, happy birthday to you, happy birthday dear Dad, happy birthday to you!"

Nate looked up at her, his face glowing in the light from the candles, and smiled so big and genuine that his happiness seemed to spill over to everyone.

"Can you believe how many candles are on it, Daddy?" Elodie asked.

"Blow them out, blow them out!" Jackson said.

Nate looked down at the baby in his arms. "Hmm. Baby or cake. Cake or baby. Tough choice here."

"I've got him, Dad," Covey said, reaching for Mason and carefully cradling him in his arms.

Tory smiled at the look on Nate's face. It didn't seem to matter how many times he was called "Dad," it always brought a beaming smile to his face. The three younger kids started calling him Dad from the moment they got engaged, but Covey had been a holdout. It wasn't until a few months after their marriage when they'd let the kids know they were going to have a new brother or sister join their family, that Covey first called him Dad.

Nate sat up straighter on the couch and Tory held the

cake out to him. He took a deep breath, closed his eyes for a moment, then opened them and blew out all the candles.

"What did you wish for?" Aspen asked.

Nate grinned. "No wish— just gratitude."

Elodie jumped onto the seat next to him, bouncing. "Gratitude for the presents you're about to get because you know we made you some great ones?"

Nate laughed his booming laugh. "Exactly."

Tory set the cake on the coffee table, and Aspen, Elodie, and Jackson raced to grab the presents. Tory kissed her baby on the forehead and smiled at Covey, then took the opportunity to slip into the empty spot on the couch next to Nate. He put his arm out and she snuggled in close and marveled at how incredible her life had become with Nate in it.

She wrapped his free hand in hers and whispered, "Happy birthday, Nate. You're the best present we could have ever asked for."

————

Author's note:

I hope you enjoyed reading Tory's and Nate's story as much as I enjoyed writing it! These characters were such a joy to spend time with.

I'm excited for you to read the next book in the Nestled Hollow series. This is a sweet and clean enemies-to-lovers romance where Alete (you met her in this book) and the new Fire Chief, Zane, get their happily ever after. You can pick their story up here.

Do you like audiobooks? I am putting more and more of my audiobooks on my YouTube channel every month. Subscribe so you'll be notified each time one releases.

May you have many hours of happy reading in your future!

—Meg

Read next:

Get your copy

They can't be in the same room without arguing--or without sparks flying.

Alete Keetch knows she is too independent, too opinionated, and too headstrong to get along with someone enough to ever get married. But that's fine by her--she gets all the fulfillment she needs by running her favorite town celebrations. Until the much-too-attractive new Fire Chief comes to town, determined to cancel them.

Zane Collins can't trust anyone but himself. When he

moves to Nestled Hollow to become the Fire Chief and prepare the town for a potential disaster, he plans to keep his heart as closed off as ever. He's not looking for any connections--he just wants to do his job of protecting the town well and use the festival money to do it.

It seems the only way he can accomplish his goals is to work with the captivating but infuriating woman who's trying to thwart his every move.

Neither one is willing to back down from what they know is right. But neither one can deny the attraction building between them. Can they get past their differences long enough to fall in love?

This is the feel-good sweet enemies romance you've been hoping for. Grab your copy here.

get the series

Coming Home to the Top of Main Street
Second Chance on the Corner of Main Street
Christmas at the End of Main Street
More than Friends in the Middle of Main Street
Love Again at the Heart of Main Street
More than Enemies on the Bridge of Main Street

about meg easton

Meg Easton is the *USA Today* bestselling author of contemporary romances and romantic comedies with fun, memorable, swoon-worthy characters, and settings you'll want to pack up and move to. She lives at the foot of a mountain with her name on it (or at least one letter of her name) in Utah. She loves gardening, bike riding, baking, swimming before the sun rises, and spending time with her husband and three kids.

She can be found online at www.megeaston.com

Sign up to receive her newsletter and stay up to date with new releases, get exclusive bonus content, and more.

If you liked this book please leave a review. Your review can help other readers find books they might fall in love with.

youtube.com/@megeastonauthor
bookbub.com/authors/meg-easton
instagram.com/megeaston_author
facebook.com/MegEastonBooks
tiktok.com/@megeaston_author